AUDITS ARE MURDER

Robert A. Clemmons

For information,
Robert A. Clemmons
raclemmo@yahoo.com

Excerpt from AUDITS ARE TERRIFYING copyright 2009

Order this book online at www.trafford.com
or email orders@trafford.com

Most Trafford titles are also available at major online book retailers.

Printed in Victoria, BC, Canada.

ISBN: 978-1-4269-1787-5

*Our mission is to efficiently provide the world's finest, most
comprehensive book publishing service, enabling every author to
experience success. To find out how to publish your book, your way, and
have it available worldwide, visit us online at www.trafford.com*

Trafford rev. 11/2/2009

 www.trafford.com

North America & international
toll-free: 1 888 232 4444 (USA & Canada)
phone: 250 383 6864 ♦ fax: 812 355 4082

ALSO BY ROBERT A. CLEMMONS

The Dan Martyn Audits:

AUDITS ARE MURDER
AUDITS ARE TERRIFYING (Coming Spring 2010)

Other Fiction:

BEYOND THE BORDERS (Coming 2010)

Dedicated to my Gwen,
My best friend, my love, my wife.

Prologue

The house was small, the garage was dusty. He had no car, no neighbors, no friends. What he had though, was a mission. He had spent the night before in the garage, going through the collection of signs he had painted over the past seven years. There were hundreds of them, stacked in neat piles against one wall of the garage. Next to them were various antique farm tools; Rakes and hoes, and in the corner, a fruit picker. It smelled of oil and dirt.

Like an executive putting together a PowerPoint presentation, he selected each sign for the next series he was about to start. Forty days, forty nights. It's scriptural. Forty signs make a complete presentation.

He selected them according to the spirit; it was clear what this presentation would be. Some of the signs were not exactly right; he would have to paint over some of the old words in order to make it fit the situation.

Today's sign needed no alteration. This one started every series. It was straight out of King James. Proverbs 31:32. You don't mess with King James. It read:

> "If you have been foolish
> in exalting yourself,
> Or if you have devised evil
> Put your hand on your mouth."

The letters were black, though he used red paint to accent the words "put your" and the second "your." He picked up sign one in the series and put it on the table next to his bicycle, and grabbed his duffle bag. He mounted the bike, slung the duffle on his back, and took off, grabbing the sign off the table with his left hand as he rode by.

No need to put down the door of the garage. The spring was broken anyway. No one ever came by here; a forgotten shack in the foothills of Bee Canyon. It had been used by farm workers during the fruit boom. Now it was abandoned, and he made it his.

It wasn't easy, but after several years of practice, he had found a way to balance himself on his old yellow bicycle while carrying the sign of the day. Today he would begin again, in a new location.

He really didn't have any idea when he started out where he was going to set up. He never did know whenever he started a series. Today, the Spirit seemed to draw him toward Santa Ana.

Sure. That makes sense. Something bad is happening there. I can feel it. They need to hear the message. They need it badly.

The sun was just starting to come up over Saddleback by the time he got to where Irvine Boulevard turned to 17th Street. This was the edge of town, just past Tustin. He felt the need to go deeper into the heart of Santa Ana. Grand? Maybe at the DMV corner. No. By the college.

Perfect.

The sun struck his ruddy red cheeks fully as he settled into his new home. The bike was behind the bushes, the duffle at his side, the sign in front. His head peeked over the top of the sign.

Today, a new batch of commuters would begin reading, and learn.

Chapter 1

Corina Zavala was beautiful. She was young, Latina, and incredibly smart. Her eyes were enormous and dark brown, almost black, and her thick black hair cascaded around her perfectly almond shaped face, gracefully edging her temples with the fine wisps of youth. At five foot-eight, she always got looks of approval when she entered a room. But her demeanor was even more striking. Everyone adored Corina, and justly so, for Corina had a gift of intensity, love and loyalty to her friends. Everyone was good, from Corina's point of view. Every one of her friends, in her eyes, was destined for greatness. Each of them would thrive, now that they were getting out of high school and entering the work force. A few of them, like her, might even be able to get some higher education.

Corina was lucky too, because her mother, Adeline, worked for a local Christian College, and as such, was eligible to receive nearly a full scholarship. Corina worked hard during her high-school years, balancing working at Drive-Out Cleaners after school hours, and studying late nights. Between work, her school, and occasionally babysitting her three younger brothers, she managed to eke out grades that won her 75% of her first year tuition. A second church scholarship was also found for Corina by Pastor Ricardo Cruz, of Iglesia de Dios.

In sad commentary on the state of California marriages, Corina's family was unusual. Although her birth father was long gone, her mother had remarried when Corina was very small, and what was so unusual was that the family remained intact and loving. Corina's stepfather, Luis Zavala, had been a hardworking man, and his dedication to his upholstery trade probably had as much influence in fashioning her work ethic as anything else. When it came time for adoption, there was no doubt in Corina's mind that she wanted to take on her stepfather's last name. Luis was 100% her father, and she never regretted having him in her life.

Luis was likewise proud of his stepdaughter. To him, Corina was as perfect a daughter as anyone could hope. So it was that tonight, the night of her graduation from Santa Ana High School, that Luis felt she deserved special recognition. All of the family had been invited to celebrate, and many borrowed tables had been circled in their back yard to display a feast. Corina had also invited only her closest friends as well; that swelled the number to only about 100 people! Everyone loved Corina. Everyone loved her familia. The Zavala house was a house of much happiness.

The party started at 6:00 pm, but Corina's friends started arriving as early as 5:30. At 4:00, Corina had left work, (Jimmy gave her the last two hours of her shift off for the party), and ran some errands, including a stop at the Drug-co pharmacy on 17th across from Santa Ana College, getting home just about that same time that her friends were arriving.

"Hola, Corina, where have you been?" shouted Theresa, Corina's closest friend. Corina paused to talk with her friend, and led her inside.

Theresa was a somewhat dull girl, both in conversation and motor skills, but she had taken to Corina ever since moving to Orange County in the 5th grade. Corina never noticed Theresa's flaws, and insisted they remain close even after Theresa dropped out of school in the eleventh grade.

Convinced that Carlo, her boyfriend was going to love and take care of her forever, Theresa gave her innocence, and Carlo gave her the slip. Alone and pregnant, Theresa remained at home, and the baby that frightened Carlo away never materialized. Lots of possible explanations were the topic of conversations, including miscarriage, abortion, or that Theresa had simply just lied to Carlo, and had never been pregnant.

In the meantime, Theresa tried her best to make it on her own. She had landed a job at Main Place mall in a health foods store, working full time as a cashier. She contributed regularly to her parent's home expenses, and really seemed to be enjoying the new directions in her life.

Whatever the case, everyone knew not to bring up the pregnancy story to Corina. She wanted nothing to do with gossip about her best friend, and if Corina had ever known what really happened, she kept quiet about it.

"Hurry, Mija," greeted Luis. "Your mother and I were getting worried about you."

"I'm sorry, I just had some things to take care of on the way home. What I need more than anything right now is some water."

Corina went to the kitchen, still holding her purchases, and emerged shortly thereafter. Luis, thought Corina might have looked a little drawn, but drawn on Corina would look positively radiant on anyone else. She gave no indication that she was tired, and so Luis assumed she looked harried from her the exertion of running all of her errands.

By seven o'clock, the party was in full swing. Ramon had arrived about 5:30, much to Luis' chagrin. To Luis, no one, of course, would be good enough for Corina, but Ramon was far from the quality Luis had hoped Corina would become close with. Ramon was secretive and while never overtly rude to Luis, would occasionally fail to greet the parents whenever he and Corina were together. Adeline dismissed it. "Most kids these days don't know how to act," she would tell Luis. That excuse didn't cut it with Luis, and it was more than obvious that he was less than pleased with Corina's choice of friends; especially Ramon Guttierez.

Music blared from the stereo; the children of the family danced under the dense trees. A gentle black Australian Shepherd mix worked the crowd with sharp ears and a hungry demeanor, even though he had already eaten a king's ransom in generous offering and spilled plates. Food filled, beverages flowed, and in the merriment, there was no sign of conflicts that can often arise at large inner-city gatherings. Mixing in with a number of Corina's friends, the mood was merry and respectful... in fact, a lot like Corina herself.

Adeline had prepared her family's favorite dessert, a cake recipe that had been handed down through the generations and had become one of Corina's favorites. She had actually prepared two large sheet cake versions over the past week, to take care of the anticipated crowd. Any gathering that involved Corina was by definition large and all-inclusive.

At 8:00, while there was still sunlight available in the June sky, Adeline and Luis brought out the cakes to present congratulations to the guest of honor. Corina was not in the back yard, nor was Ramon and so Luis went into the house to search for his "Mija," his beloved stepdaughter.

What he discovered in Corina's bedroom hit Luis harder than an iron fist. He fell to his knees, wailing. The Shepherd's ears twisted as his cries shattered the evening air, and silenced the crowd outside. Adeline dropped the plate she was serving and ran to his side. She too, was shattered.

No words would be appropriate to describe Corina's current state. To say she was dead just didn't seem right. Corina couldn't be dead: Could a princess ever not be awakened? Even though her soul had left the shell of her body, Corina was still encased in beauty. In death, she lay, as beautiful as when alive; except for the dullness in her eyes. Corina's body reclined on her bed, as if she had just sat down briefly, and lay back toward her pillow to rest for a brief moment. Had her eyes been closed, you would believe that with a word, she would rise up in an instant.

One of the more insightful crime lab techs later waxed poetically. Only her eyes held the secret. Only her eyes revealed that life was gone. Seemingly without reason, the lovely Corina was gone; her heart simply stopped beating. She left behind only the shell that once caressed a life of beauty.

Chapter 2

The area that was once the open fields of the Sepulveda land grant is now is an intricate and orderly grid of lace. If you view the area on an aerial photograph, you are struck with how unbending the original community designers were. Straight lines cross straight lines at regular intervals. The major streets became major streets almost as an afterthought, and when city planners decided more room was needed to handle more traffic, they chopped off chunks of property from homeowners on the edge, leaving their walls only feet away from the curb.

Newer community planners got a little wiser and laid out Irvine, Mission Viejo and Laguna Hills with a softer lace made with more curves, property set-backs, and wider main arteries. Live and learn. But the grid lace of Santa Ana extend up off the map. The windows on those old houses, now just feet away from Bristol, are covered with window bars. The area became less desirable, as prettier and newer communities sprang up to the south. Families moved out of those chopped off properties, and so the city allowed small businesses to set up shop in them. Palm readers set up shop next to dentists, businesses moved in with less pride in outside appearances than your typical homeowner.

The cross streets are dark, even during the day. In June, the sun shines just a little dirtier here than most of the rest of Orange County. The jacaranda trees that line the streets have become enormous canopies blocking the sun, dropping nearby freeway dust down with their purple flowers and tiny, lace-like leaves. Living in Santa Ana is to live with dirty lace. Finding your place on the lace, and finding a way out of the dark grid, isn't an easy thing to do.

I get to see those lacy patterns a lot. My office shares space with our campus environmental planning group, and what would environmental planning be without aerial photographs? The other day, as I was weighing how I was ever going to get through the drudgery of writing my cashiering audit report, I found myself pondering the pattern of Orange County streets. On the lower right corner of the photograph sat our main campus, a gem of a place, a green eye on Orange County's troubled face. To the northwest sat the straight grids of Santa Ana. In the east, were the foothills leading to Saddleback Mountain with new, curvy developments molding themselves to the rounded foothills. Rancho Santa Margarita and Ladera Ranch are the newest incarnations of community planning, Orange County-style. Smack dab in the middle of the photograph sat the old El Toro Marine base, the source of OC's current scowl. Now they are calling it "The Great Park." Only time will tell if the millions of dollars dumped into the land will make the toxic land mass anything close to a park.

A closer photograph let me identify individual properties. This one was taken from another direction, with our campus at the bottom and the beach cities toward the top. Here, the grids follow the coastline. Upscale shopping malls dominate the landscape. Over here, you can make out the Newport Peninsula and Balboa Island.

The island is made up of hundreds of home lots even tinier than those in Santa Ana, but what a world of difference. Here, the houses build up to the property edge, with wide open windows inviting island strollers to voyeuristically join the occupants as they eat dinner and watch TV. Here, bars on windows would be more than a travesty; you'd be considered just plain gauche.

I was just finishing up my last audit. It seems the head of cashiering at a sister campus managed to tuck about $10,000 a day in university receipts into her purse every night for about six months, and when their auditors discovered it, the Regents got a little upset. Immediately, all the campuses in our system had to go through an exhaustive audit of all our cashiering functions, even though our campus had just completed one about the same time Hilda up north started tucking university bucks into her private account. It was time to start a new project now, and I was ready to rid myself of anything cash oriented.

Little things excite us auditors.

Usually, we don't find many juicy tidbits. By and large, people pretty much do the right thing. Occasionally, and I stress, very rarely, do we find anything really meaty.

Then someone (not us, I assure you), leaks it to the Orange County Gazette, and those enterprising reporters take the credit for our work, gets a Pulitzer, while one of us gets demoted or canned. The ever wise administrators assume we're the ones who leaked the info. Trust me; the last thing an auditor wants is the press butting in. But I love living on the edge.

The result is our little gem-of-a-green-eye winds up blackened with print ink. And in turn, our work gets a little harder, because... duh... no one likes to talk to auditors anyway.

"Thinking of moving, Martyn?"

I hadn't realized Marvin had joined me by my side. Marvin Gardner (yes, that's his real name, and no, he hates Monopoly), was, by my guess, about six years my senior and had been named head of audit about five years ago. Marvin is a man of great ethical character, and he and I have become good friends. That's fortunate, especially when he catches me daydreaming instead of writing.

"Sure," I said. "I was picking out my future house on Balboa." I'm quite the wit.

See, that's sort of funny to us locals, because there's no way anyone on an auditor's salary working for the State of California could ever afford to live in even a back room on Balboa, let alone own a house. Maybe Hilda would consider sharing her new-found wealth.

"Ha," said Marvin. Marvin never overdoes it laughing. "OK, when you get a minute, come on in, because I have a new assignment for you."

I finished up a lovely Excel spreadsheet showing the various areas of risk cashiering faced. I wanted to rate "seeing too damn much of the auditors" as their number one risk, but satisfied myself instead by creating the Mona Lisa of spreadsheets. By the time I was done, I had a masterpiece. It was another lovely grid of color. Then I realized I was looking at grids again, and so I figured I needed to get up from my desk for something new. I walked down the hall to Marvin's office. He was wearing a white shirt that was leaning toward yellow, just like the Monopoly property group, with his sleeves rolled up a fold or two, a Jerry Garcia tie hung loosely on an open collar.

Marvin's space was only slightly larger than mine. You may think this strange, but the University has some very specific rules, not the least of which is how big someone's office is, depending on rank. So, believe it or not, someone actually sat down and came up with measurement standards for offices. Why? Because if Dr. Earock is operating a really big research project from an office the size of Versailles, and Dr. Ahard is operating a really big project from a teeny, tiny office, some Department Chair somewhere is going to be stuck in a fight between Earock and Ahard space.

Both Marvin and his office can best be described as "stacks." The filing system makes perfectly good sense to him. Lord help anyone else. I wedged myself in the chair in the corner by the vertical blinds as Marvin plopped a familiar file down in front of me. It was our risk-ranking file, which contained the findings of our campus wide risk assessment that we performed at the beginning of the fiscal year.

Unlike business, it's common for us to count beans annually, starting in July and ending in June. It's easier, if you consider how Universities operate on a school year basis, starting in September. That gives us three months to get our act together before the students arrive, and look like we know what we are doing.

Our Audit department is no exception, at the beginning of the year, we take a survey to rank departmental risks, take top ten riskiest areas.

"Before we do this thing again, we've got a few things to clear up. This cashier thing really got us behind," Marvin said. "We've got about three more weeks until fiscal end to sew up the last three audits. If you and LaVonne can take Pediatrics, I'll give Core Services to Ronnie and Bruce to do a speedy review of Parking/Special Events. With any luck, we'll complete the year's assignments, and we can start next year on time."

"Maybe," I said, but in my head I thought three weeks isn't exactly a whole lot of time, in audit terms. It can be done, depending on how cooperative your business unit is, but I hate to whine.

I'd been in Pediatrics before, and Karen Taylor, their Business Officer, was both cooperative and sexy. Cooperative was good, sexy was to be ignored, because this was, after all, a public institution, and the last thing you want anyone to know is your internal lusty thoughts about them. Sexual harassment charges take many ugly forms and a long time to iron out. Funny, how an appreciation for one individual's beauty can easily turn into something pretty ugly for many. Enough creeps sitting on the edge of women's desks and saying things like "I need to see a doctor to keep up with you, honey," have made life hell for the rest of us, who just appreciate non-males in the work force.

Don't worry. I'll mind my P's and Q's. Working with Karen would be an appreciable end to an otherwise dull year. I called her and set up an appointment for that afternoon.

Chapter 3

The University has a pretty odd and shaky relationship with our Medical Center a couple of cities to the north. Originally a County Hospital, the County of Orange decided they had poured enough money into the indigent drug emergency business, and magnanimously passed the hospital over to University management. The University was all happy teeth and glad hands with the prospect; the hospital group resented the takeover. There was already enough competition for the limited hospital resources, and now sharing them with a bunch of university-types was not acceptable. You can only take so many x-rays per machine per day. Now decades later, you'd think the staff at the Medical Center would get over the takeover, but no such luck. Even though most of the original individuals have retired by now, they have passed the resentment culture on to their successors.

Fortunately, there are a few more mature individuals in the system, and by the year 2455, things should work out fine. Karen Taylor is one of those individuals. There is never a good time for an audit, so we usually have to have some pretty thick skin whenever we meet resistance. Karen offers none. Don't go there.

LaVonne and I grabbed a bite at the In-N-Out across the street, and then cut through John Wayne International for a shortcut to the northbound 55 freeway. LaVonne Fontaine has worked here just about as long as I have, and over the years, we've become good friends. Short and, shall we say, very full figured, LaVonne is a good auditor with a mischievous manner and a very private private life.

"Well," she teased. "I'll bet you're none too sorry to pull the Pediatrics audit."

I played dumb and asked, with big puppy-dog eyes, what on earth did she mean.

"You know dang well what I mean," said my friend. "I know you always have the hots for Karen Taylor."

"Why LaVonne, you know I'm nothing if not professional, at every given moment."

"Yeah Dan, I'll give you that. You're a pinnacle of good behavior. Too damn good, if you ask me. You're so good, every mom on this campus hopes their teen boy grows up to be you. Do you have any idea how you effect women on this campus?"

"Well, they do tend to swoon whenever I tell them I'm coming over to audit them."

"An audit isn't what they want, 'Cool Hand Dan.' You know, sometimes, it wouldn't be such a bad thing if you let one or two of them know you are interested."

I felt the better part of valor was to keep my mouth shut, so I said "LaVonne, I just don't think it's a good idea to develop relationships with the people I audit. Conflict of interest? If I responded the way I'd like to respond half the time, two things would happen. One, I'd be setting our office up for having improper relationships with one of our control points, and two, I could jeopardize my career here, over unwanted advances."

"Don't worry about that, pal," LaVonne quipped. "I doubt if there were a single female soul on campus that wouldn't respond to any sign from you. Hell. Half the married ones would like to pinch your cheeks, and I don't mean the ones by your nose. You couldn't give an unwanted advance if you tried. Your good, you're ethical, you're handsome, you're funny."

"I'm hurt," I said. "I was hoping 'smart' would be in there somewhere."

"O.K., you do have one major flaw," LaVonne replied, just to let me sweat out my compliment fishing. Then, after a beat, "You're also a smartass."

Being two people in one car, we took the elevated carpool transition lane to the north 5. Go north to take the north 5. No wonder tourists get lost here.

"What are you so surly about?" I asked.

"I dunno. I just had a bad weekend," she said.

"Your son ride his bike off the roof again?" I prodded.

"No," she replied, and then reflected. "You'd think that at 28 he'd be brighter than that, wouldn't you? No, he still has the cast on, and gravity has a way of wrecking bicycles falling from 12 feet carrying a large moron."

"Motherhood throws you all sorts of moments of pride."

"Yeah, I guess. Anyway, I suppose my mood is just based on something I heard this morning. One of my neighbors lost a daughter last Friday."

"Really?" I said with distance. "Accident?"

"Well, what's weird," LaVonne continued, "is that they really don't know." They were throwing a party for her graduation, and somehow, she just laid down and died."

"Jeez. Some party."

"No kidding. Anyway, her mother is just a mess, and her father is even worse, and so far no one is saying why she died. Everyone assumes it probably had something to do with her sleazy boyfriend. He disappeared right about the time she was found. But the thing is, she was really a together kid."

"Did you know her well?"

"Well, not really. Her mother and I were both involved together in our kid's school PTA. Our street is pretty tight. Self preservation."

LaVonne was referring to the gang activity in Santa Ana. About every seven years the Police do a sweeping shakedown of the area to weed out and prosecute gang activity, but that's about as effective as bailing water with a spoon.

We pulled off the 5 Freeway and turned left. People complain a lot about the Southern California Freeways, but I'm a big fan. They go everywhere you want to go, and don't go where you don't want to go. That's because cities in the LA basin that didn't have the foresight to see how important freeways were going to be in the future fought having them cut through their communities. Consequently, the cities that are best served by the freeways are the ones that either allowed the planners to cut through the middle of them in the early stages, or the destinations grew up around the freeway. Orange County falls mostly in the latter group. Anaheim was just a collection of German farmers and field workers until Mickey Mouse made his home right off the then-new Santa Ana Freeway, Interstate 5. When Walt opened the front gates, that was essentially as far as the 5 went. Eventually it wove its way through the orange groves to San Diego, and those of us who grew up here back then long for those days before everyone moved here from the east. You think Californians are crazy? That's because you probably don't know any. The real Californians were decent, hard-working people. They built ranches and farms and made a desert into a garden. Then television was invented, and everyone spending a cold winter in the east saw a warm oasis on the west coast while watching the Rose Parade, and suddenly, we were inundated with new "Californians."

There was a dirt parking lot off to the right; in recent months they saw fit to pave it. It was one of the few places you could park on University business and not have to pay for parking. We crossed kitty-corner to the Med Center, and found our way to Pediatrics.

The lobby was one of the more colorful reception areas at the University. Apparently some student got the creative juices flowing, and painted murals on the wall with a "Under the Big Top" theme. I greeted the receptionist, and told her we had an appointment with Karen. She wrinkled her nose when LaVonne and I handed her our cards. Nose-wrinkling is a light version of Auditor Revulsion. While LaVonne was admiring a semi-portrait of Emmett Kelly, I was taking in the painting of an enormous African elephant on the west wall (now that he resided in an American circus, would that be an African-American elephant?). I couldn't help but wonder if the receptionist considered herself the ringmaster. "Ladies and Gentlemen, Boys and Girls. In the Center ring: the Doctor will see you now."

She returned with permission to enter the inner sanctum, and I twisted one of the juggler's balls to open the door. Sorry. I was giddy doing something other than number crunching.

What can I say? Karen looked, and smelled, divine. Ralph Lauren, I think. A tall leggy blonde in a dark blue business suit, Karen's perfect teeth gave us a welcome smile that could melt butter. She ushered us to her office, a stark contrast in neatness to The "Under the Big Top" theme. I put on my charming but all business face, and together the three of us worked out an audit plan. Karen's desk was glass. Perfect for sneaking peaks at her very fine calves. Sometimes, I am ashamed of myself.

Chapter 4

"*I saw you looking at her, Dan*"
　　　"*What are you talking about?*"
"*Karen. I saw you looking. It's alright, you know.*"
"*Not yet, Amanda, Not yet.*"
"*You know, what LaVonne was saying is true. You are an attractive man.*"
"*I know you think so, but it embarrasses me.*"
"*Why?*"
"*I don't like thinking about me. I don't like thinking about me in... situations.*"
"*Like romance?*"
"*Like Romance.*"
"*I'm not coming home, Dan.*"
"*You might.*"
"*There are things.*"
"*I know. I wasn't what you wanted.*"
"*No. Yes. I don't know. There were many things.*"
"*I suppose I know that too. It wasn't all me, was it?*"

"No... I'm not even sure it was you at all."

"Then what?"

"I had to leave, that's all I knew."

"Are you alright? I worry."

"I know you do. I worry about you too. I want you to go on."

"I still can't."

"But you must. It is time."

"You didn't answer my question. Are you alright?"

There was no answer.

Chapter 5

I would place a real money bet that no one, in the history of mankind, ever said as a child "when I grow up, I want to be an auditor." Just about all of us got into it through the back door. In fact, our office doesn't really have a front door. University space is at a premium, and as the place grows, (it has grown a lot lately), departments get shuffled to and fro, and probably more frequently with non-education University entities. Audit got plunked down in the back corner of our Business Services group, which includes the aforementioned Campus Planning group. They have the offices up front; auditors please move to the rear.

I came into audit as honestly as anyone else; I could no longer do my old job. Not that I'm some old, disabled coot, but a pistol shot to my left knee put my police career to an end. I have a noticeably affected gait, but I can get around well enough. It's just that I can no longer leap over tall buildings in a single bound. The elevator works just fine, thanks.

A friend of mine, Tom Kamens, was working here back then, and he's the one that suggested I apply at the University. I came, I saw the ad, I conquered the interview. Apparently they had just gone through an audit of the Campus Police Department, and had some difficulty doing it, since cops have this tendency to keep sealed lips around outsiders asking questions. I was just the right unskilled guy at the right time.

Marvin hired me; he figured anyone can be taught to be an auditor; but breaking the police barrier could be useful. Every once in a while... and I mean a rare while, Audit has to call on the good assistance of our staff in blue to secure documents and evidence in instances where a cover-up might take place. By having a former cop on staff, Marvin figured we might be able to develop a "better working relationship" with Campus Police.

Veni, Vidi, Vinci.

Over the years, I've gotten pretty good at audit skills, if I do say so myself. Having a partner like LaVonne helps. I picked up plenty of techniques from Marv, and he sent me to a bunch of seminars by the IIA, which stands for the Institute of Internal Auditors. I suppose they formed the institute after a bunch of auditors, who had been told they should be institutionalized by several of their clients, took their advice. Their main office is in Florida, so I envision this bunch of retired guys sitting around in loud camp shirts, figuring out where they want to vacation next. "Hey Harv. I need to visit my sister in San Francisco. Let's do a seminar there." For some reason, none of those guys seem to have a reason to travel to Los Angeles, and rarer still, Orange County.

Now that I think about it, a lot of people still ignore Orange County. The county that spawned Richard Nixon, Disneyland, Charles Keating, and also went bankrupt during the eighties, is one of the fastest growing areas of the world, one of the most powerful business areas, and one of the least reported. Just about all the traffic reports on L.A. radio stations conveniently forget to advise about jams on our OC freeways.

Cities in Orange County don't count to most local news organizations; far be it to report about our inner cities. We are considered too conservative to even have an inner-city. Valiantly trying to fill the void in news coverage, the Orange County Gazette is the paper of choice in most OC driveways. Miffed that we've been snubbed for so long by L.A. media, Orange County-ites reject by a margin of two-to-one the encroachment of any Los Angeles-based rag.

I picked up the latest issue from the driveway of my modest-but-overpriced condo, off Trabuco in Irvine. There was nothing of real interest in the first section, from what I could garner from its current folded state. Shar, my neighbor, was just getting home from work. No one else in our building knows anything about Shar, as if they sense something they don't want to know. But Shar and I do talk, and if you're clever using Yahoo, it doesn't take a whole lot of time or investigative skills to discover Shar's web site. Many conservative Orange County males, who are computer illiterate but horny as hell, have utilized Shar's services. Sweet little bedroom community of Irvine; if only you knew who lived next door.

I gave a nod to her, she gave a weary wave back, and I returned inside to my breakfast on my patio. On page one of the community section, a little weasel reporter I knew, by the name of Scott Thomason, has picked up on the story of LaVonne's neighbor. It would have been merciful to the family if they hadn't run a photo of the girl, Corina Zavala, but Thomason made every heart-tugging connection his un-unbiased journalistic heart could find. The girl was a very pretty girl, and her picture, taken straight from the graduating class pages of the Santa Ana High School yearbook, showed a girl who had direction and joy. A pretty unusual combination, if you've taken a look in most inner-city high school annuals lately.

The article talked a lot about the pain of her family and friends, and said very little about what killed her. It only described the way her body was found; lying on her back, on her bed, as if to rest. It sometimes is true: investigations on cases for minorities get less attention.

Her funeral was scheduled for Friday afternoon. In lieu of flowers, the article mentioned the family's wish for people to make donations to a scholarship fund at LaMont Christian College, where the dead girl was planning to attend in the fall, and where the mother was currently employed. I envied LaMont; being a small, private institution, they could set up a memorial scholarship fund in very short notice. Our University would take forever. Corina would be dust before it got established properly. Slow wheel turning can drive you nuts sometimes.

Reading the story of a young girl with everything going for her, cut down before she even had a chance to live, made me sick. I didn't feel like finishing breakfast, so I put the dishes in the dishwasher, went into my garage, and took off for the Medical Center.

One last comment about Orange County: We're quickly running out of orange trees. On my way to the freeway, which is really only two long blocks away, I passed five former fields that were recently denuded of groves, in the interest of coming events. One is already a golf driving range. Just to make sure the county always had at least one citrus tree for future generations, I rescued one from a nursery during a going-out-of-business sale, and put it in a pot on my back porch.

Young Orange County has grown up, and the pristine fields of yore have given way to massive developments. Youth is so often wasted on progress.

Chapter 6

Karen Taylor had efficiently gathered most of the materials LaVonne and I had asked for, and introduced us to Rayce Skyler, a homely, bug-eyed boy who held the enviable position of Administrative Assistant I. He was to be available to us to show us whatever we wanted. Rayce was probably about 26, but was really good at projecting immaturity before his years. How he ever got a job working for Karen was beyond me. I thought Karen was sharper than to hire a geek like this. It was only after a few hours that I discovered Rayce's talent. In spite of his idiotic first impression, he really produced excellent documentation.

We also met the other players. Connie Marwick was the office manager. Irene Pedroza was nurse. Rita La Masters was the receptionist we met yesterday. I was right. Even her name said she was the ringmaster.

We met two of the four doctors. Dr. Adam Bolo was department chair, and you couldn't ask for a more capable man to trust with your child's health. Dr. Carlton Cambridge was running on high speed from room to room. Two others, Linda Wrightwood and Ty Renaeta rounded out the official Doctor list.

In addition, Manuel Maravilla served as Physician's Assistant. He seemed to be everywhere, both preceding and following the doctors with every appointment. His shirt pocket was filled with a pen, a box of Good and Plenty, and a Hershey Bar. With all that running around, I figure he needed the energy. There were also a couple of students from time to time that we never actually met.

I took a random sampling of Pediatrics billings. Every single one was picture perfect. Just for luck, I took another sample. It isn't in any Audit book, but I like to make sure. No problems with the second sample either. At this rate, if I get this done in two weeks, I can take a week off before we do the Risk Ranking.

LaVonne was checking out the filing system. You can get in lots of trouble in medical education if your files are out of order. The Joint Commission of Higher Medical Education will effectively third degree burn your buns if your files are incomplete.

Someone brought in a baby with the cough that had to go all the way down to his toes. Another mother brought in her twins for immunizations. All day long, there was a parade of moms and offspring, with a variety of ills. One kid whacked his head at the skateboard park across the street from the Med Center. Rayce commented that that happens on a daily basis; one of the two unsolicited remarks ol' bug-eyes made all day.

The other occurred at day's end.

I was reviewing time cards. Good as Karen's systems were, I was having some trouble reconciling everyone's hours. Some people, like Connie, punched in and out like clockwork. I guess, since they used a time clock, it was clockwork. You decide.

Other people seemed to have several hours of ghost time. Some were here, according to the time cards, even though the Medical Center Employment records showed they had called in sick. Those kind of things always give us fits. Was someone in the Medical Center just making a mistake, or was someone punching in for someone else. If so, why would they do that?

The Doctors didn't punch in. It really didn't matter. Their job classification didn't require it. Irene, the nurse, was inconsistent in her cards. So was Physician's Assistant, Manuel Maravilla. Ringmaster Rita was just plain old sloppy.

I was finally able to decode Rita's time, and after a couple of hours, everything jived just fine. It was coming up to the end of the day, so I was putting things away where I could get them tomorrow. Because of my bum leg, I was somewhat hanging on the side of the chair, a little out of sight, putting the cards in order in a drawer box. All of the patients were gone, as were the doctors.

Suddenly, Manuel Maravilla burst out of one of the rooms and started yelling, nay, screaming at Rayce (does anyone say "Nay," anymore)? Somehow the x-rays Manuel had called for had never arrived, and he was willing to toss all dignity aside to call Rayce all sorts of names, blaming him for the discrepancy. Assuming the two of them were alone (the rest of the crew had just left) Rayce was the first person Manuel saw when he came out of the office, and was therefore the recipient of all the verbal abuse. I was the second.

I came up from behind the desk, and Maravilla clapped shut. He slammed a file down on the countertop and stomped out the door. My guess was that this guy was so steamed, the Hershey bar in his pocket was probably fondue by now.

LaVonne came out from the file room with her briefcase; ready to go but primarily to check out the commotion. Rayce turned to me with a sheepish look. He gathered up his belongings, and we all quietly headed to the door. Rayce then offered his second voluntary comment.

"That son-of-a-bitch. I wish he was dead."

Chapter 7

"**W**ow. Is that guy a hothead or what?" said LaVonne, as we walked to the car.

One thing I've learned in both the Audit biz as well as Police work is that the real story is usually much larger than the one you see.

"Well, it was the end of the day," I offered, "and my guess is, at the rate of speed Maravilla operates at, he probably gathers a lot of stress in eight hours."

"I hope he can go home and have a healthy hit of Schnapps then. That guy needs to relax!"

I thought about referring him to Shar, my neighbor. Her website has lots of details about her massage techniques. I quickly dismissed it, considering her other talents. I could be arrested as a pimp.

"So," I said, "What are your plans tonight?"

"Hold on, loverboy. I know I was lecturing you about asking people out yesterday, but I never imagined you'd pick on plump little me."

Actually, LaVonne is a very attractive woman, for as much of her as there is. Her eyes twinkle, and I enjoy her banter. In fact, her tone was banter. She and I have visited many a dining establishment. Besides, I wanted to talk with her about Pediatrics.

I ignored her feigned flirt. "I just thought we could compare notes over adult beverages and dinner."

"Always a bridesmaid, never a bride. Yeah. That works for me. Tell you what. We're close to my house. Why don't you follow me home, I can drop off my car, and we can leave from there."

We got in our respective cars, and headed south toward Santa Ana. A turn on Memory Lane, and then a right on Bristol, and we were getting close. We made another right, and then a left on Poplar, which, strangely enough, was lined with Jacaranda trees.

LaVonne pulled into the driveway of her house; a blue bungalow with white trim, neat rose beds in front and a garage in back. She checked her mailbox, ran it inside, dumped some food into her cat's dish, and we were on our way.

About four blocks down, on the other side of the street, your attention was drawn to a truly amazing sight. I knew who lived there in a minute. Or, more appropriately, who no longer lived there. In spite of the helpful instructions for donations to LaMont College, there must have been hundreds of bouquets of flowers laid side by side on the lawn of a beige home. There were posters and gifts, candles brought by hundreds of fellow classmates, colorful flags and bright mylar balloons and pinwheels. A banner, staked behind the flowers, was half hidden. The message, in blue tempra, was clear and clean.

"Corina - Vaya con Dios"

Chapter 8

We turned left at the end of Poplar, returned to Bristol and hung a right. I glanced over at LaVonne, and she was crying.

"It's just so damn unfair," she quietly sobbed.

"You knew the girl well," I asked?

"Well in a way. Corina grew up on our street, and I've seen her for years. Now it seem so strange that she is gone. Her mother and I would talk shop from time to time. She works for LaMont College in Anaheim, and when she found out I worked for the University, it was as if we were immediate friends. It's going to be tough to see her on Friday."

"What's going on Friday?" I asked.

"The family is having sort of a memorial gathering at the house, and Adeline asked if I would come. I feel so awful going to those kind of things alone."

"Do you want company?"

"You offering?"

"Yeah. There's something about this whole thing that intrigues me. A girl dies, no one knows why yet. the coroner will figure it out eventually, but since there was no violence, it won't be a priority. Plus, it means a lot to you. Gosh," I said, giving her my best boyscout grin, "I'm here to serve."

"Seriously Dan, that would really be great. You sure you don't mind?"

"What are pals for?"

LaVonne got really quiet after that, and I couldn't think of much else to say, so I patted her hand with mine. I could have tried to say something, but nothing seemed sufficient. Death came knocking in LaVonne's neighborhood, and found a pretty young girl at home. Then I saw the sign.

No, I wasn't listening to a radio station playing Ace of Base. On the corner of 17th and Bristol, by the old Monkey Ward shopping center, sat a red-faced man whom I had seen before. He wore a pink polo shirt, some old safari pants, and an Australian Bush hat. In front of him, he was holding a sign, about three feet tall and five feet wide; white with big black letters. The sign read;

"Bad Boy Security
You're not as safe as you think."

LaVonne stirred from her melancholy at the sight of him.

"Great. Now just what the hell is that supposed to mean?"

"Haven't you ever seen him?" I asked. That guy's all over the place. I've seen him for years. In fact, for a while, he was on campus. Where were you?"

"Nope, he's new to me. What's that sign all about? Is he a nut case?

"Maybe," I said. "But probably more like just a little left of eccentric. He finds a street corner, and he's got a whole series of signs he goes through. I've seen him early morning and as late as 10:00 p.m."

"10:00? That's pretty late. So where have you seen him?"

"Oh, for a while, he was on a corner by my house," I said, glad to have something else to chat about than the fate of Corina Zavala. It's a religious thing, I think... at least, that's what I get from the signs."

"That one didn't seem very religious to me," she said. "What did it say? 'Bad Boy Security?' What's that?"

"Well, near as I can tell, most of his signs are somewhere between "conspiracy theory" and "conservative religious-political" themes, if I'm reading them right. That one, I've seen before. I'm guessing he's making some sort of commentary about the sad state of our social systems, and putting our trust in government."

I glanced over at LaVonne. She had that look on her face you see on a stunned deer, just as your headlights catch them. Any minute, I thought she was going to jump from the car, from my crazy preaching. I tried to explain.

"If you watch him carefully, the signs start to make sense."

"I think you're the one getting a little left of eccentric," LaVonne returned. So how many signs does he have? Do you remember any others?"

"Well, the local throwaway paper that comes out on Thursday's in my neighborhood did an article on him," I told her. "Apparently, he's got a place to stay, but doesn't turn down offers for sleep-over digs. He stays on a corner for forty days, and I remember his final sign has the word "Goodbye." I've seen him in Newport, Irvine, and Tustin, but for some reason I just never expected to see him this far west. He rides a bike in, sign under his arm, from God knows where."

"Kinda like seeing an old friend, Dan?"

"Yeah. All my friends hang out on street corners."

Or at least guys I knew. After Viet Nam, a lot of my fellow military men and women had a hard time assimilating the senselessness of that stupid mess, and from time to time, you see one or two meandering in alley's and public places. I've even heard them referred to as Nam-vets, which smacks of a total lack of compassion to me. Those guys were boys thrust into a nightmare; boys like me. Most of us survived, although the terror still remains deep in our brains. Whether the sign man ever served in Nam or not, I sure understood his distrust of political promises. I guess that's why I could relate to his sign, and LaVonne couldn't. And maybe that made me a little left of eccentric too, but I'd rather be that kind of crazy than crazy as the political idiots who orchestrated that fiasco.

Melancholy seemed to be the theme of the evening, so I figured we needed something a little upbeat. I passed Sunflower and turned right into the parking lot at South

Coast Plaza. I found a spot not too far from my goal, and LaVonne and I found our way into The 19th Hole.

The place is a loud and tall appendage on the east side of the mall. Its two story layout is accented with red wood and leather seats, while a sweeping staircase takes you from the singles pick-up haven below to the dining tables above. During the summer it hops with tourists who are fans of the pro-golfers and actors who own the joint. Regardless of when you come, it's always busy, with the buzz of people bouncing off the wood and young secretaries with loud laughs trying to attract young attorneys' attention.

We lucked out, and got a table in the open-air terrace. I ordered a Sam Adams, LaVonne chose a Margarita.

"So, are you getting anywhere in the filing system," I asked?

LaVonne leaned toward me as she spoke, to compensate for the noise.

"Doing pretty good," she reported. "I'm half way through my samples, and nineteen times out of twenty, things are all complete and documented.

"Nineteen out of twenty? What kind of problems are the twentieth?"

"Near as I can tell, the numbers on the prescription pads don't go consecutively."

"That's not usually a problem," I said, but it usually isn't a problem because prescriptions pads aren't often numbered. Some medical offices add a control to number the prescriptions, just to keep track of them, but even then they don't necessarily get filed in order. Tracking them from chart to chart is heady stuff, as each Doctor bounces from visiting room to visiting room. Whenever they need a new pad, they just grab the most convenient one. Even if the prescription is numbered, real life practices make it hard to put together a complete sequence. The only real way to track them is if the prescription pad is the kind that makes a duplicate, like those kind of check books. Then the office can verify if all pads are accounted for. Pediatrics had duplicate books. LaVonne was going to try tracking down the errant pads tomorrow.

Our conversation went on like this for a while. It's riveting stuff, if you're a guy in Florida wearing a cheap Hawaiian shirt trying to figure out where your next seminar will be. For the rest of you though, I understand it can be kind of dry.

LaVonne ordered dinner, and our conversations became less business and more friendship. Her stunt-impaired son had called the night before from New Mexico and informed her that his latest trick was to become a father. Becoming a grandmother was not in LaVonne's immediate plans, but he was well beyond an age where she could make decisions for him. Fatherhood is a big responsibility, and the Bad Boy was about to have to face up to being a man.

Somehow, the invincible youth was about to discover true vulnerability. Just as Corina's parents were reminded so painfully that their secure family could be shattered by death, and LaVonne found that her son's actions were beyond her own control, LaVonne's son was soon to face the worries of mortality with the life of a child in his care. His Bad Boy Security was in for a lesson. He wasn't as secure as he thought.

Chapter 9

S*ummer is better. Less rain, more traffic. It's hot. Doesn't matter to me. There's just more people. That's the important thing. More People.*

Do I care what they think? No, but yes in a way, because the message gets lost. Labels. They label me, and then think that takes care of things. Not fair. Gotta get the message across. They'll see. They'll come around eventually.

Summer's hot, but I have protections. Ozone a problem, so I keep covered. Still, can't help it. Face gets burned pretty bad. It's worth it though. It's my life. I can do with it as I please and I choose to please the cause. His message. That's the important thing. The burnt skin, doesn't matter.

Yes. Got a place to live. Always get shelter. Don't need much, and I have some money. Check comes every month. Like clockwork. You can count on it. Like me. You can count on me. Got to get the message out, and the message is what counts.

Where? Not far. About twenty minutes on bike. It's an easy trip, and I move around. Keeps it interesting. Sometimes the city, sometimes the neighborhoods. Eventually, I'll reach everyone. And I'll still be here, until they understand. It's important.

Oh, where do the messages come from? Depends. They come. Most I've used before. Sometimes I paint new ones. Depends. Each night it comes to me which one.

Family? Any of us really have family? I doubt it. That's why I'm here. Family needs to be saved. It's gone now. We had it. We lost it. The message needs to get out.

Friends? Lots of familiar faces. They wave. Some gesture. I'm beyond that. Doesn't matter to me. They're the reason I do it. I have to be here. Dependable. They don't understand it. They need to. Maybe I can convince them, because nothing has been stable. I'm stable. I'm here. 40 day, and then a new location, all over again. 40 Days. Like Noah. It's scriptural.

The message? If I had to say one thing, it's to pay attention. We live with heartbeats. We just exist. We can do more. Do you like today's sign? That's the message. We act secure. We think we know, but we don't. Our lives aren't living. We need to really live.

Love. No. Never had it. Need it, but never. I know what people think, but the message. that's what's important. Teach the people. Make them think. Stir them to life. That's the important thing. I'll be here.

Honk your horn if you like me. Honk if you think I am crazy. Honk me, Honk you.

Summer is better. More people. When it rains, they stay inside. Not me. I'll be here.

Chapter 10

It was a fitful night of sleep. Too many things were coming home to roost. I guess I never got over the melancholy of the previous night's observations, and so I needed to get up and get wet in the pool.

After all these years, it still hurts. I swung out of bed and staggered a bit when my leg gave me it's usual protest. I got ready for the pool and put on my University terry robe and grabbed the association pool key off the rack by the back door. Shar's car was still missing, which meant she will probably be meeting her association dues payment this month, so that she too can enjoy the benefits of poolside recreation.

Thoughts of Shar providing poolside recreation were washed away as soon as my body hit the water. There are many schools of thought as to how warm an association should keep their swimming pools. My association was of the "warm enough to just keep icicles from forming" school. I suppose the theory is that in order to keep algae from growing and proliferating, you freeze its nards off. I pondered briefly if algae have nards.

Naturally, whenever you have a public pool next to human habitats, for some reason the folks who don't like early morning swimmers seem to choose the condos that are most near the pool. That's why Mrs. Barrington was giving me the evil eye as my body slapped down in the water this morning. I ignored her as usual, and on my next lap, I came up for air just long enough to notice she had shut her vertical blinds in an ineffective effort to make me go away.

I swam to wake me up, I swam to loosen up my aching body. I swam to clear my head, and today it was filled with all kinds of thoughts; both sanguine and sublime. Having a job where you run into the likes of Karen Taylor was one of the more sublime thoughts. Corina Zavala was one of the sadder ones. I find it interesting how sometimes a news story can get under your skin. I never knew the girl, but maybe because she lived close to one of my friends, I found myself reflecting on her tragic end. Usually, I wouldn't give a story of similar ilk more than a minutes thought, and now that I reflect on that, that's pretty tragic in itself. Every day, the papers are filled with stories that mean tragedy to someone. Yet somehow, most of us manage to keep it at some distance. The fact that the Corina story was getting to me was telling me something about myself. What was it about her death that struck a familiar chord?

Maybe it was Amanda.

As I made another turn at the pool's edge to change directions for the fourteenth time, my thoughts turned to my Amanda for the millionth time. Amanda was my world at one time. Then she was gone. Like Corina, Amanda was gone without explanation. We had been married for nine years, and then she was gone. It was the mystery I could never solve.

I just came home one December day, and Amanda was gone. She had taken some items, but left most of her things, and slipped detection wherever she went in her Jetta. Everything else was just as they had been that morning when I kissed her goodbye. She gave me no hint of unhappiness; at least that I was sharp enough to detect, and because of that, I suspected foul play right off. But after months of investigation, Missing Persons had no leads; although I think one or two investigators actually suspected me of foul play.

Eventually, they found Amanda's Jetta in New Hampshire, of all places. It was clean; no evidence that anyone other than Amanda had been in it. It had been parked at a local supermarket for a week. My hopes were high, but the trail went dead again. No witnesses, no patterns, no leads, and more importantly, no Amanda.

Every cop is Columbo. Family, friends, business associates (Amanda worked at a law firm in Newport): not a single soul ever heard from her again. Maybe she ran off and joined a cult.

"It happens," said Detective Newsom. "Sometimes the rubber band inside a person just goes zing, and they go and seldom return.

I once read this case of a guy in England who disappeared off and on for months, sometimes years at a time. The last time he was gone for nearly two years, only to turn up as a ringmaster for a circus in Ireland.

Seems the guy has this rare disease, and if he's left without some family member to ground him into his present, he actually forgets who he is, his family, the fact that he even has a family, and he goes off to live a new life."

Did Amanda forget our life together, or was she taken? I never found out. The one thing I do know is that I didn't kill her. She just left, with a lot of evidence that she had been in my life, as a reminder that she had been real and not a dream. Is she alive? I hope so, every morning when I wake and every late night I finally crash to sleep. I think of her every quiet meal I eat alone, and with every beer I share with Marv, and every lap I swim.

The fact that there was no final solution makes it harder. She's maybe alive, probably dead. It is so weird; I'm the one who went to Viet Nam, but my wife wound up MIA. Without knowing, I'm still hanging.

Corina's parents have a different circumstance, but understand, I'm not saying what they are experiencing is any easier, just because they had a body to prove she was gone. Loss is loss, and whether you've lost someone to death, divorce, neglect, or simple absence, like Amanda, there is no difference. You are always faced with the question, "How do I go on from here?"

For myself, I'm kind of just feeling my way along. I sold her Jetta a couple of years ago. The kid who bought it couldn't believe the low, low mileage! If only he knew what kind of mileage was really involved. I smiled a big grin and waved as he drove it away, and then went inside and crumbled to the floor, wailing my eyes out. I didn't get up again until the next morning.

Swimming is good. It washes over you and cleanses you, and the chlorine burns your eyes, and you feel baptized into a new creation every day you emerge from the pool. My life goes on, and even though it doesn't always seem to make sense to the casual observer, I've managed to carve out a reason to go on, and a code of ethics to live by. I now firmly believe that there is a way that life ought to be lived, and I dedicate my life to pursuing it, in Amanda's name.

Somewhere out there may be a woman who ran off, and just forgot, and who may wake up one day, and remember. When she does, I'll be ready.

There. That's fifty laps. Time to go.

Chapter 11

On my way to work, the subject of Corina Zavala came up again. This time, it was courtesy of the news. Sometime late the preceding night, Ramon Guttierez had been arrested in connection with a local drug bust. Normally, reporters don't reveal names in generic, twenty-second news stories, but when they found out this kid had been the boyfriend of Corina Zavala, it was too good to pass up. Their implication was clear; was Ramon's link to drugs somehow the cause of Corina's death? The Coroner's office was still "looking into it." Knowing how news reporter's embellish their stories with non-factual statements like "they're looking into it," I've got a feeling the Coronor's office didn't really give the accusation legs with such an irresponsible statement, but that's the way it came across. Evidently, that's how they teach kids these days in Journalism charm school.

I met LaVonne at the Starbucks near our office and then we struck out for the Medical Center. It was a typical audit day; the kind of stuff that gets dinner party conversation going full tilt. LaVonne did some more work tracking the prescription books, and had most of them accounted-for (prepositions are OK for the end of a sentence if hyphenated to the preceding word). Still, and too often, there was a break in the pad numerical sequence that couldn't be traced.

I reviewed more of the office records. You may find it interesting to note that the patient records were off limits to me. That's actually OK. You see, there are standards that make it illegal for me to view medical charts. Those charts are confidential records of individual health histories, and as such, are classified as confidential documents. Only attending physicians and may poke their noses in them, with emphasis on the word "attending." Even if you're a doctor, you can't peruse files for your own personal research or pleasure. You have to have a reason to be in those files, and the patient has to give permission for anyone to peruse the green sheets. Taking information from your file is as sacred as taking your liver. If you don't give your permission for a doctor to review your file, you have a legal case.

In the front of each medical file are green sheets of paper, where Doctors are supposed to write supplemental notes every time they order a test, write a prescription, or make some brilliant diagnosis. They also review the charts at day's end and then talk into a transcribing machine, summarizing visit, which is then transcribed by an outside company and included in the file. That's why the green sheets are important; they remind the Doctor what transpired so they can give detailed descriptions in the tapes.

What I am allowed to audit is the system the office utilizes to track those files, and I discovered a few were out of place or missing. I took a random sample of names from the billings, and then checked to see if the corresponding record was in its proper place. In most cases, they were. Most were checked out with a check-out card in its place. Unfortunately, one or two were not in the slot where they should have been.

I hate it when that happens.

Rayce hated it even more. The panic attack he was going through was bugging his eyes out even more than usual. He looked like a muppet that was afraid of being eaten.

"I don't understand it," he flustered. Nothing's supposed to be taken without filling out a check out card. What was the name on the second file?"

"Velasquez," I answered. "The first one was Gallegos."

Rayce got this little look on his Kermit-like face for a tenth of a second like he suddenly had some brilliant insight, but it was gone even faster. He seemed to be searching for all the possibilities in his geeky head. If he had been a thermometer, I'd bet money that his bulb would burst. Actually, I think I burst his bulb anyway, because he was so proud of his filing system. It seemed incongruous that he'd be missing records. He was so thorough with everything else.

"Has this ever happened before?" I asked, but Rayce was evasive.

"Usually we can put our fingers right on the file in a second's notice." Then he lowered his voice and murmured, "Have you told Connie or Karen yet?"

"No. I just now found... or didn't find them. I thought you might have a good reason. Let me take a second sample, and we'll see what turns up. Then maybe we'll have a better picture to take to them. In the mean time, why don't you see what you can find."

My second swipe at it revealed one more missing file. One out of 100 doesn't sound bad, unless you happen to be that particular patient and need medication immediately. In the course of one hour, we discovered three patients who, as far as the medical file knew, were billed for no services rendered.

I checked in a few offices, Doctors Bolo, Wrightwood and Renata. No files. The first two physicians were in surgery today, and Renata was on vacation. That might have explained where the files were, except there still should have been a check-out card. Besides, the missing files were for closed cases. Physician assistant Manuel Maravilla was also out, although he was scheduled to be in the office. PA's don't always assist in surgery. Things seemed a little loose around Pediatrics, and it was really getting under my skin. LaVonne and I left at five, leaving Rayce behind to brew in his stew.

Chapter 12

The next day was set aside for research. LaVonne had a class in the morning that was required for her Government Audit certifications, and so that left me in the archives pulling out old audit reports. I found the one I had done in Pediatrics two years earlier, and a couple of other historical documents that, if anything, documented a clear progression from mismanagement to a healthy state of affairs under Karen Taylor's guidance. Karen had been moved to Pediatrics after being in OB/Gyn, and I thought about the implications of how Karen's career followed the life cycle; from pregnancy to raising kids. What's next for her; Geriatrics?

Pediatrics had been in bad need of a good financial manager. They had severe losses before Karen came on board. Audits revealed that Karen revamped the tracking system for insurance billings, and made significant inroads in improving Pediatrics financial portrait. In the last three years, Pediatrics had been turning a tidy profit, gradually making up for the losses her predecessor had incurred.

I'm supposed to be impartial, but I felt bad about uncovering the filing errors. That's a serious violation, and I hoped Rayce was able to come up with good explanations for the missing records. I gave him a call after lunch.

"Yes, I was able to find them," he confirmed. "Miste... uh, I was able to find them, along with a couple of other files, and get them back in place."

"Had they just been misfiled," I asked?

"Well, er, no. One of our people took them out without signing a check out card. They were in his office."

I hung up, glad that Rayce had found them, but I was surprised he found them in someone's office. Granted, I didn't go through drawers, but it seemed incomplete. I would have to put it all in my report and I'd have to tell Karen on Monday.

Just before 3:00 I had arranged to meet Lavonne in Santa Ana, at the church for Corina's funeral.

"Thanks for coming," LaVonne greeted me, and she took my arm as we headed for the door. "Did you have any trouble finding the place?

"Finding it, no," I said. "But parking was a different matter." Iglesia del Dios was located on 17th Street, and was part of a small converted business building that had white painted glass windows in front, and virtually no parking lot. You could pull in on the side of the building, but there was only room for about ten cars along the side. Most of the churches congregation walked there from surrounding blocks, and there was limited parking on the adjacent streets. I found a spot about three blocks south and 1 block east of the address on 17th.

The sidewalk in front was a throng of family and friends, but I cringed to see the van from OC Today about a block down. The cable news network found Corina's funeral newsworthy. With the arrest of her boyfriend, Corina was fast becoming the most famous dead girl in Orange County.

I spied a few other news ringers in the crowd. It would have been easier if they had worn the hats with press cards in them, like the old Superman TV show, but having been at the University, I had become familiar with a couple of the local journalists. Scott Thomason showed up, and my old newshound pal from my precinct days, Melanie Minkhoff, was now a reporter for OC Today.

A tall, classy woman dressed in black approached us. She was clearly closely associated with the proceedings.

"LaVonne!" she cried, and LaVonne and the woman hugged for a few seconds. From my point of view, I could see the outpouring of affection surprised LaVonne too.

"Adeline," LaVonne managed to stammer, "I... I'm so sorry." The hug happened again, a little more brief, and then LaVonne managed to turn her friend toward me and introduced me. "Adeline, I'd like you to meet my friend Dan Martyn. Dan, this is Adeline Zavala - Corina's mother."

"Hello," I said, and Adeline regained her composure. I gave my condolences, and we walked toward the church entrance.

A voice that reminded me somewhat of a shrill little dog caught my ear to the left.

"Martyn! What are you doing here? Friend of the family?"

"Hello Scotty," I said as I turned reluctantly to the little runt reporter. I knew this little mongrel and I didn't much care for him. Can you tell? Wedding, funeral, mall opening or university scandal, Thomason always looked the same. He slouched about five feet eight inches, and always wore tan, wrinkled khakis, gray Hush Puppies, and a shirt/tie combination that reminded you of Alfalfa trying to get all dressed up. His greasy hair laid flat on his head, and he had this little sneer that as much said "I'm a jaded reporter... what do you do?" He didn't even do anything yet and I wanted to dope-slap him.

I could just read the little guy's little mind. He knew me, he saw me with the deceased's mother, and so he was going to work through me to try to get to her. "Pulitzer Prize, here I come." See why I hate this guy?

Sure enough, he latched on to the three of us like we were part of the same litter. I felt Adeline tense up next to me as you might expect anyone who has just had their personal tragedy thrown to the wolves.

"C'mon, Dan, talk to me," Thomason pushed.

"Not now, Scotty. Not now." I could see he wasn't going to give up when all of a sudden, a second voice came over the din.

"Thomason. Back off."

It was Melanie. Now for some reason, Melanie has always intimidated the hell out of Thomason, and when she spoke to him, He whirled with a fierceness, but gave up the chase. Mind you, this all happened within seconds, and as I was turning my body to block Thomason from Adeline, I saw he was already cowering away, and my eye caught Melanie's, who had moved directly behind him. My glance to her said "thanks," hers said "on behalf of the Orange County Media, I am so sorry," and LaVonne and I escorted Adeline through the doors.

Safe inside, we were met at the door by Adeline's husband, Luis, and the Pastor of Iglesia del Dios, Ricardo Cruz. LaVonne and I took a seat to the left, as Cruz and the Zavalas walked down the side of the church to some seats up front. Gradually the room filled with mourners, and respectfully, the reporters remained outside. This was fast becoming a media zoo, and even though I didn't like the Zavala's having to go through the hassle, I was glad that for once, the University was not at the heart of this media storm.

Chapter 13

I don't care much for funerals, but then again, who does? As funeral's go, I was extremely moved. This was no dispassionate speech about ashes to ashes: Clearly Corina was well known to "Pastor Ric." As the service progressed (there was no body in sight), it became clear that Corina was a remarkable young girl. Active in her community, her short life "yielded much fruit," as Pastor Ric put it. Whenever the church had a need for a volunteer, Corina was the first on the list. Whenever friends needed an open ear, Corina was available. She worked hard, studied hard, and gave of herself in every positive way imaginable.

"You have heard it said, " Pastor Ric expounded, "that the secret of living isn't the amount of time in your life, but instead the amount of life in your time. Corina was truly the one they had in mind. Though we are left with the tragedy and loss of no longer having Corina among us, we can also rejoice that God did give us the gift of Corina for even a short while. There is not one in this room whom Corina did not somehow touch or inspire in some way."

I thought about that for a minute. I was, if anyone was, the one person in the room who would have been the exception. Then again, maybe not. I couldn't deny that in the past few days, just knowing of Corina had been sufficient to sway my thoughts and emotions. Somehow, even in death, this young girl touched hearts and stirred people to reflect on the value of life. To Corina, life was clearly God's most precious gift, and in a world that seems to have lost appreciation for that value, Corina had served as a light to bring people back to their belief.

Few enjoy a funeral although I hear it has been done. Even so, I was beginning to dread the end of this one, because I knew what lay outside for the bereaved. I leaned over to LaVonne. "I think we need an exit plan."

"I agree, but what can we do?"

"Actually, I'm really only worried about one of those guys outside."

"Thomason?"

"Right. If I take care of him, do you think you can get a ride back to the Zavalas?"

"Sure. I'll ask Eileen and Johann. They're right over there, and live next door to me."

The choir began singing an upbeat gospel number, which seem a little incongruous to me because you don't often hear gospel songs sung in Spanish. I made my way down the outside aisle and stepped out the side door that emptied in a narrow walkway between buildings. There was a wood pallet to navigate past, and clearly someone had recently used the walkway recently in an experiment to kill weeds using human urine, but I managed to make my way out front.

There weren't many of them; OC Today had set up a shot across the street with Melanie's back to the church awaiting her cue for a live remote. She'd be tied up there. Besides, I wasn't really worried about her. Melanie at least exercised taste and class in her reporting.

Another reporter I didn't recognize was just packing up; He appeared to be from a local Spanish language radio station (his car had the name of it on the side), and he was just about to pull away. He had already gotten the quotes he needed with the attendees walking in. The good news was that the funeral had been scheduled for late afternoon, and so most broadcasts wouldn't have time to file a new story prior to airtime at 5:00 pm. The Zavala's lucked out. The end of their funeral was "broadcast inconvenient."

That left snotty Scotty, the print journalist, who laid poised with microphone in hand to waylay the first body to come out the front door. That was just like Scotty. He didn't even work for a news organization that did broadcasting. He was a writer, but he fancied himself the ultimate reporter, and from his point of view, reporters used microphones. The idiot actually thought he was Mike Wallace. And they say watching TV doesn't make you stupid.

I acted casual, as if I had come out for a breath of air. I ignored Thomason, and leaned against the front of the building. It didn't take the mongrel long.

"Dan Martyn!"

I opened one eye against the afternoon sun and gave him my smile of tolerance, without saying a word. He was used to that.

"Martyn. How are you connected to all of this?"

I opened my eyes, and gave him the once over.

"Oh, Scott, I'm really just here with a friend. No connection whatsoever."

"C'mon Martyn," he urged. "I know you too well. What's the tie in here?"

I laughed a fake gust of wind, and shook my head.

"You never give up, do you Scott?"

Thomason was proud of himself. He was getting me to chat.

"Nope. I know a story when I smell one. Why did the University send two of its auditors to attend a high-school girl's funeral?"

Damn. He recognized LaVonne too. Now I was walking the edge.

"Look, Scott. It's useless talking to you. Take it from me. I'm here because LaVonne knows the family as a neighbor. That's all"

Thomason got a gleam in his eye. He was sure there was more. Just what he had in mind, I have no idea, but now I was even more determined to distract him.

I looked down the street in both directions, as if I was checking if I was being watched.

"OK. Scotty. Because we're old friends. I'd love to give you a scoop."

"Really?"

"Yeah, sure. Can you wait here for a second? I'll get my car."

Thomason looked like he was about to out-newspaper Bob Woodward.

"No way, Martyn. You'll leave me cooling my heels. I'm going with you."

"That's really not necessary... "

"I insist. Where's your car?"

I led him east and south to my car. I ignored his digs along the way, saying I didn't want to talk so publicly. I got in and unlocked the doors. Thomason scooted in the passenger side.

I drove back to 17th, and headed toward Tustin. A couple miles down the road, I pulled into a strip mall and got out. Thomason followed. There was a Baskin-Robbins, so I led him in, and got in line. It was a hot day so there were four others in line ahead of me. I figured the service was just now getting out.

"Jeez, Martyn. What gives? First, you don't want to talk, then you do, then you don't want to talk in public, then you drag me here to a crowded ice cream store. What the hell are you thinking?"

"I never said I wanted to talk."

"Yes you did. You said you wanted to give me a scoop."

The look on his face when he realized what he just said was priceless. He was now far away from his story, and he knew he wasn't going to get one from me. I grinned.

"I do want to give you a scoop. What flavor would you like?"

The words that next came out of his mouth were certainly unfit for a family ice cream parlor. He stomped out the door and began a furious pace back to the church. He missed the curb as he stormed into the parking lot, and twisted his ankle as he fell to the ground. The epithets were flying fast and furiously. There was no way he was going to get his in-the-face story now.

My job here was done. But I ordered a double Mint Chip on a cone anyway.

Chapter 14

I left Thomason rolling around in the oily asphalt and hooked back up with LaVonne at the Zavala home. In lieu of a graveside ceremony, the family opted to just have friends and neighbors over.   There were lots of cars, so I parked at LaVonne's and walked on down, figuring I'd probably escort LaVonne home anyway.

Talk at the gathering was centered, of course, around Corina's death, albeit in hushed tones, especially any time the Zavalas were nearby. The Coronor's office had decided that she died of an unidentified drug interaction, and that in addition to the drug charge Ramon was already facing, the DA was looking to make a solid connection that would implicate Ramon in Corina's death as well. Evidently, the real reason there had been no body at the funeral, or a graveside service, was because she had not yet been released.

This was quite a twist of events to everyone to consider, myself included.   It was one thing for a young girl to die without apparent reason. Now there was a whole new, sinister shade to the story. Corina may have been murdered. As bad as her early demise was, considering it was murder made it even worse.

Several of Corina's friends who had been present the night she died were in attendance. For many of them, it was a difficult replay of the events of that night, and they nervously speculated about Corina's final hours and Ramon leaving the party early.

One girl, named Theresa, cornered me and talked my ear off about how Corina had been instrumental in motivating her to get a job, even driving her to the interview. Others talked about how Corina helped them with certain subjects at school, or assisted them when they needed an extra hand watching their siblings.

Just then Theresa turned a little too quickly to greet someone else, and knocked my elbow. It jiggled my hand just enough to get coffee on it, hitting my shirt without really spilling on the floor. I looked up and saw LaVonne headed my way with Corina's stepfather, Luis. He was older than I expected; His thick head of black curly hair had been invaded by the whitest of white hair on his temples, and he had a long, distinguishing white moustache that curled at the ends and gave you the impression of a jolly walrus. He was short and stout, but not out of shape; his frame was one of strength. His eyes were the key to his emotional state; They were red and weary but looked directly at mine when LaVonne introduced us.

"Dan Martyn. I am glad to meet you. Welcome to our home."

"Thank you, Mr. Zavala. Please accept my heartfelt condolences..."

"Luis, please," he corrected me.

"Thank you, Luis." I made a weak attempt to extend our conversation. "If there is anything I can do to help you or your family, please let me know."

"I just may take you up on that," he responded, politely.

"Dan and I are partners in our investigations," explained LaVonne.

"Investigations? Are you police detectives?" he asked a little suspiciously. Apparently he did not know LaVonne as well as Adeline did.

"No, no," I assured him, and explained how we were auditors at the University. That seemed to satisfy the topic, and he excused himself to attend to other guests.

"I don't know about this," LaVonne confided. "The mood here seems really weird, now that this thing has taken an uglier turn."

"Yeah, I know what you mean. Look, I have to wash before this coffee stain on my cuff gets worse. Do you want to leave?"

"Sure. Why don't you find the bathroom and I'll seek out Adeline and tell her goodbye."

We agreed to meet out front, and just off the hall to the entryway I located a small bathroom that served as both a guest bath and the two bedrooms adjacent to it. I stepped inside and closed the door, and ran some water on my cuff to try to lift the coffee. Just as I was doing that, my eyes scanned the top of the sink, and there were a number of girl-type items. Apparently this had also served as Corina's bathroom.

In the corner below the medicine cabinet were perfume bottles, a small gray container with Chinese writing on it, and a medicine bottle. It was oriented just so one particular feature caught my eye. I picked it up, and examined the label more closely.

I quickly got my notepad out of my pocket and jotted down the prescription number, and the pharmacy where the prescription had been filled. If what I was thinking were true, it could mean that the little weasel I left rolling around in the Baskin-Robbins parking lot may sniff out the big story he was looking for after all.

Chapter 15

The Bones are just one of several gangs in Orange County, and don't fool yourself. This bastion of tan bodies, rich properties, and famous housewives isn't the bubble people tend to think it to be. OC has it's share of trouble, and gangs are just a part of it.

You can drive down the freeway in just about any metropolitan area, and see walls covered in graffiti, but not so much in Orange County, because the Supervisors of the County are well aware of where their power originates. Orange County is all about image, about promoting the bubble, and about symbolism. To the visitor, graffiti means gang trouble, so we spend lots and lots of money in public works to remove any hint of it. Walls are built with ficus growing on it, so no one could tag it if they wanted to.

The ultimate irony in Orange County happened at the site of the Great Park development. The very first thing they put in was this enormous, orange, balloon to take visitors 500 feet up in the air over the former Marine airbase. Though there was nothing yet to see from up there, the symbolism was appropriate. Hot air, and a big bubble. But I digress.

Gangs do exist here, and often very dangerously. There is a permanent curfew in cities like Santa Ana, and anyone displaying any sort of affiliation with a gang can be arrested and jailed immediately. Again, looks good, but doesn't get rid of the problem.

The problem is drugs; lots and lots of drugs. Orange county is affluent, and affluence means parents with lots of money. Rich parents beget rich kids, and rich kids means peer pressure galore. If you aren't the fastest, or smartest, or prettiest, or have any issue of low self-esteem at all, the drug culture is quick to attract.

It's the gangs that make the drug world turn. There is lots of money to be made, and territories are fought over. Law enforcement has to spend thousands and thousands of hours fighting it. It is like Hercules fighting the Hydra. Cut off a head here, and two more pop up somewhere else.

All it takes is a single contact. One kid who uses convinces another kid that crystal meth will help them excel. The trouble is, it works at least the first couple of times. Meth gives the kid a feeling of confidence, efficiency, and on top of the world.

It's the off times that suck. Anger. Paranoia. Rage. Parents never want to believe it, and they think their kids are just being teens. But by the time they figure it out, they are in too deep.

The first use fries a few brain cells, and so subsequent uses never seem to quite attain the same original high.

So the kid uses it more often. Combines it with other things.

Gangs use this, and one other tool: Sex. As the kids get swept into the world, they find themselves rejected by their old friends. They alienate themselves, and can only find comfort with their contact. They become as addicted to the person as the drug, and will do whatever they are asked. Deliver packages. "Borrow" a car. Meet someone in a hotel. Have sex with them. Have sex with others.

It doesn't take long for the terror to take over their lives. And the drug industry thrives.

Gangs formed originally for a sense of protection, almost like a club, more than anything else. It was brother with brother, neighborhood united in neighborhood. Memberships lasted lifetimes, and new generations were inducted, even as illegal activities increased. Old members became mentors to the new kids joining. It became like a family. Fathers and sons, Uncles and nephews.

The Bones owned the area of Santa Ana that surrounded Corina Zavala's neighborhood, but they didn't often ply their wares on friends. There were richer areas to mine. They would go to parties in more affluent areas. Make one contact, with one well-to-do kid in Rancho Santa Margarita, and you could have yourself a field-day. Arrange a garage party, when the folks are out of town, and friends of their friends will want to hook up for the thrill of being with someone "dangerous." Murderous would be more appropriate a term. The sweet, rich daddy's girls become hooked, and families are destroyed.

Other gangs concentrated on the young professionals. Occasionally, you could even find a tech firm executive who embraced the 70's love for highs. Most of these guys made so much money, so quickly, they built empires around them to protect their excessive lifestyle. If you could get an executive for a customer, you were on easy street indeed. Your chances of being caught were reduced. Now you could simply pose as a businessman at a power lunch, and feel more secure knowing powerful executives are good at keeping secrets. Secrets are the name of the game in the tech world.

All the gangs shared two things: The lust for quick wealth, and total disdain for their customers. The execs were fools, working hours upon end to get their hit, and then hours to avoid paying taxes on it. Gang boys got paid quickly, in cash. The teen kids were disposable. Once they got diseased, strung out, or perhaps even dead, end of problem. Drop them. There are more to find elsewhere, each one of them thinking they are different than the rest, that they can handle it. Idiots all, but they pay good.

Corina had known Ramon all her life. She went to school with him when he was just a funny, scrawny kid at Santiago Elementary School. All through their education, they kept in contact. In an area where lots of kids are transient students, Corina and Ramon grew up in the Santa Ana Unified School System, going to Francis Willard Intermediate, and finally Santa Ana High.

Corina first met Theresa at Willard, when they were teamed together for a science report. They became fast friends, sharing hopes and dreams, just as any other young girls.

In High School, Ramon began to distance himself. Corina was not fond of his new friends, and asked him frequently to do thing other than spend time with them.

But Ramon was resolute. He liked these new guys, who made him feel important, instead of little and scrawny.

As her education became more and more important to Corina, it became less and less important to Ramon. At 16, he pretty much mailed in his school attendance. But Corina still found time for he neighborhood friend, and through some resolute determination, managed to keep him close enough to remain friends, and far enough to be nothing more.

Ramon was soon in the business of partying, and discovered the wonderful world of sex in short order. But he knew to never try anything with Corina. She was the one person who liked him, not for what he could do for you, but just for who he was. It was uncommon, a line never to be crossed, and he compartmentalized his relationship with her. She was clearly someone different. Not sex. But someone worth more. Someone he respected. Someone he loved.

Chapter 16

"**W**hat's the matter?"
        "Nothing."
"'Nothing' my wooden leg. Something's bugging you, Dan."

"Maybe, but so what?"

"So what? You actually said, so what?"

"Sew buttons on your underwear."

"C'mon, Dan. You haven't said a word to for two blocks."

"Clearly, I don't want to say."

"Men."

LaVonne and I reached her house. She walked up two steps to the side door that led to her kitchen. She opened the door with her key and turned to look at me.

I looked back. I didn't turn to leave.

We just stood there. Me in my thoughts, her waiting patiently.

"I think we might have a problem."

LaVonne closed the door again and sat on the concrete step.

"I think the University might have had something to do with Corina."

LaVonne looked at me incredulously.

"How?"

I pulled my notebook out and turned to the page I wrote in Corina's bathroom. I showed her the prescription. LaVonne looked at it passively.

"What's that?"

"Information off of a prescription bottle I found in the Zavala's bathroom."

"What did you do, raid the medicine cabinet?"

"No," I explained. It was sitting out in the open. Sort of."

"Sort of?"

"It was behind a bottle of perfume."

"Oh. So what's this got to do with us?"

"The Doctor who wrote the prescription. He works for us."

"Who?"

"Adam Bolo."

"From Pediatrics? That Adam Bolo? How do you know?"

"Because that's why I picked up the bottle. I saw his name as I washed my cuff."

"Who, I am afraid to ask, was the prescription for?"

"Corina Zavala."

The weight of her name settled on receptive ears. LaVonne thought for a moment.

"Why would a Pediatrics doctor write a prescription for an adult?"

"Well, it really might not be that unusual," I answered. "After all, she was only eighteen. She could have gone to him for years. It's just..."

"Just what?"

"Well," I started, "I just don't recall seeing the name 'Corina Zavala in any of our records."

"And are you familiar with all our records?"

"Well, no," I answered, "but it seems like I would have noticed this one. Remember, I was trying to locate files with Rayce yesterday, and I took samples of the billings? There weren't that many "Z" patients, and since Corina Zavala has been on my mind lately, I think I would have noticed."

"Are you sure?"

"No, I'm not. That's why I didn't want to say anything."

LaVonne sat for a minute and thought. I mulled it over for a bit too. We just sat and stood there. Then LaVonne said, "Maybe it's just another clerical error. Maybe she never got billed. That's why you didn't see her name."

"If so, where is her file?"

Would there be one if she wasn't billed?"

"If Dr. Bolo wrote her a prescription, he would have made a green sheet note of it, and would have recorded his action to be transcribed into a file. Where's her file?"

More silence. I finally broke it.

"Something's wrong here."

I turned to go. I turned back. LaVonne was far away.

"Yeah," she said. "Something could definitely be wrong."

Chapter 17

The trouble with finding problems late on a Friday night is that you have to wait until Monday to do anything about it. I thought I'd better let Marv know, so the next morning I called his house. He wasn't there, his wife said. Could she take a message?

It was then that I realized I had never met Mrs. Gardner. What was her name? Ava? Organic? I couldn't say I remembered. Marv and I would have an occasional brew, but I don't think I ever heard him say her name. It was always "The Wife." I would always fight the urge to respond by saying "Which wife?" I would imagine that if she knew, Mrs. Gardner would just about have a cow, knowing that Marv was referring to her like an object. The Car. The House. The Wife. Then again, maybe she was used to it. It was better than "The Little Woman," I suppose, but not much. Maybe she called him "The Husband." "The Little Man?"

"Yeah," he'd say "The wife and I are going to Temecula this weekend. She really likes to poke around their antique stores. I like to stop by the wineries. You should try Leonesse. They are actually good!"

He and "The Wife" were always doing something interesting. "The Wife" took him to a play at the Performing Arts Center. He'd take "The Wife" to the movies. I imagine they probably saw a movie called "The Wife." Some sort of Italian film that won for Best Foreign Film. "Isabella Rosalini is: "The Wife."

I identified myself, and "The Wife" recognized my voice like we were old pals (Herbal Gardner? Rock?). Now I really felt ashamed. It was too late to say "...and what was your name again...?" Until I had a chance to check with Marvin, I'd have to just avoid her name altogether. I asked her if Marv would be back soon, but she said she doubted it. She didn't offer to tell me what he was doing, so I didn't ask. I just left my phone number. Marvin's spouse said she would have him call.

I decided I needed some fresh air. I went next door. Shar was home. When she came to the door, she was wearing a pink jumper over some sort of body suit thing. It had lacy arms and lacy legs. The jumper had script print of French words. She looked like she could put a big dent in some Orange County dork's pocketbook in a quick hurry. She smelled of men's cologne. It was actually her idea. By wearing men's cologne, wives and girlfriends don't get suspicious when their man comes home smelling of Old Spice instead of Estee' Lauder.

"Hi Shar. Can Zeus come out and play?"

Zeus was Shar's doberman. Zeus had a job. Keep the garage smelling funny. Every Saturday, I'd take Zeus for a stroll. Shar and I fell into the pattern one day as I watched her struggle one morning, trying to get Zeus in a cage, so she could hose out the garage. I was glad she was at least making some attempt to keep the odors down, and for the most part, Zeus was pretty well behaved. Strong, but well behaved. I offered to take him for a walk while she finished her clean up job, and she took me up on it, and after a while, it got to be a regular thing. I was more than happy to help her if it meant keeping my property from going downhill. And every once in a while, if Shar was called to, ah, assist some gentleman in cruising the Caribbean, over the weekend, I would go over and feed the monster dog as well.

So Zeus and I were pals, and Shar was grateful. I thought it was probably better to be on friendly terms with your neighbors, and it goes both ways. Sometimes, if I have to go out of town, Shar comes over to water my plants.

I know. You probably think I'm some sort of idiot. But let me tell you, I've seen a lot of crap in my days as a cop, and frankly, you get pretty sick of it, if you have any brains. I don't judge Shar. She does what she wants, and it's none of my business. Just because you sell sex for a living, it doesn't mean you can assume sex is a given. In her business, you can meet the lowest of low life, and I decided I just wasn't going to have it in my life, regardless of how pretty Shar is.

And Shar is very pretty. Originally from Argentina, she has long, beautiful black hair and perfect skin.   She can class up, or trash down, or be whatever international look you want, depending on your fantasy. But Shar is definitely hands off territory. Besides; most people deserve respect. Not all, but most. Shar got into her line of work the same way I got into mine. Neither of us aimed for what we wound up with.

"G' morning, Dan. I'll see if I can corner Zeus. Come in. You want some coffee?"

"No, no thanks Shar. So how you doin'?"

In a way, I feel more like her protector than neighbor, and so we talk. That proves I'm not dead below the waist. Taking women who sell sex for a living under our protective wings is a common hazard for those sworn to protect and serve. Even though I haven't been on the force for years, I still fall back on my cop persona.

I'm not fooling Shar, either. She knows my questions aren't just casual. She knows all-too-well that "protective mode." Both cops and customers get that way. Some customers develop father-like complexes. Others develop ownership feelings. Either way, girls like Shar develop personalities and techniques to counter the protectiveness and owner personalities. But more so, they hone protective skills to handle the bigger jerks; the owner personalities that think they can do anything they want with the object of their transaction. What's weird is sometimes, girls handle it by allowing these guys in closer. That's why guys like me get protective, and girls like Shar get big dogs.

"I'm fine, Dan, thanks." She tossed. "But thanks for asking."

True to form, Shar ignored my prying, leashed Zeus up, and soon dog and Dan were on the streets. Zeus's leash is fifteen feet long, and another three can be added if he sees a duck or rabbit and yanks my arm to full extension.

Trabuco is a wide street with a center divider that is actually a drainage ditch, albeit a rather attractive one. Water drains down a man made little riverbed lined with cut grass and eucalyptus trees. There are always ducks, and Zeus truly believes that duck would be a fine menu, if I ever let go of the leash. As we walked, I mulled over the preceding day's events. Here I led Scott Thomason on a wild goose chase, as if I didn't have a care in the world, in order to protect the Zavalas. Now it turns out that my employer may have a connection to Corina Zavala, and I've managed to anger the Orange County Gazette's jerkiest reporter.

The thing is, it doesn't really matter if anyone at the University is guilty of any wrongdoing or not. If the Gazette even takes facts like the ones here, and reports them in any light, it's going to make us look like a bunch of baboons. Fact 1, a girl dies. Fact 2, a girl dies a drug-related death. Fact 3, she has been taking drugs that were prescribed by a University Doctor. Fact 4, the University can find no record of the dead girl as a patient. Another fact may be that all of this is coincidence and that only minor clerical errors were made, but it won't matter much to the general public. Our high esteem as an institution will go right down the drain, a Doctor could lose his practice, a big lawsuit will have to be paid off, and, worse case scenario, the entire university medical center could be shut down. Granted, that's pretty extreme, but it could happen, if the Federal Government felt our organization violated enough standards to make us a risk to society. Heads could roll.

Fact 5. I'm the one who pissed off the twerp that could make it all happen.

I hope "The Wife" gets a message to "The Husband" soon.

I worked this all over several times in my head before I found myself back at Shar's place. Mission accomplished. I got exercise, and the ground was wet; Shar had hosed out the dog evidence again.

Shar had changed clothes. She was now wearing a loose Coldwater Creek white blouse with matching slacks. She was barefoot and obviously enjoying a little "me time." I left her in her reverie.

After I dropped the dog back off at Shar's, I got home and checked for messages. No call from Marv, but I did have one message that had been "left at the sound of the tone." It went something like this:

"Hello, Mr. Martyn. I met you yesterday. My name is Luis Zavala. I was wondering if my wife and I could meet with you tomorrow. Please call me at...."

Chapter 18

If this were a George Lucas movie, this would be the part where the hero says "I've got a bad feeling about this."

Common sense tells me that I should just not call. Common sense also tells me that it is highly unlikely the Zavala's have made the connection between Corina's prescription and the University. If they had, they would have known about it when I was at their house. There was nothing on the prescription bottle that would lead them to the University; chances are they wouldn't know Adam Bolo worked for us.

Common sense and the University General Counsel would agree. Don't call. Wait until we know more. But common sense has a hard time living next door to curiosity. Curiosity says "Hey! How much worse can it get?"

So I found myself dialing the phone, but not to the Zavala's home.

One ring.

Two.

"Hello?"

"Hi LaVonne. It's me, Dan."

"I had a feeling you'd be calling."

I suppose I did too. I knew the whole weekend wouldn't pass without us comparing notes at least one more time.

I told LaVonne about the phone call, and she said she knew because Luis had asked her for my number.

"Did they say what they wanted?"

"Luis said you had offered your help. He was wondering if you'd be willing to give him a hand."

"Doing what?"

"Clearing Ramon."

I thought about that for a while. "Why would they want me to clear Ramon? I'm not a cop anymore. Why would they think I could do anything?"

LaVonne said nothing.

"Oh. Oh no. Not you..."

"Believe it or not Dan, I never thought any of this would come up..."

"You told them I used to be a cop."

"I told them you used to be a cop."

"Why did you do that?"

"Well, it wasn't recently. You may find this hard to believe, but sometimes people talk to friends and neighbors and tell them about friends and people they work with..."

"Yeah, go on..."

"And so a couple of months ago I was talking to Adeline and I may have mentioned that I worked with this handsome, brilliant former detective who is now an auditor..."

I finished it for her. "And so yesterday they put two and two together, and now they want me to help them clear Ramon. One question. Why would they want to clear Ramon?"

"Because if you clear Ramon, you'll clear up Corina's reputation."

"How's that?"

"Think about it. They don't know about the pills you found. They really don't suspect the University of anything. As far as they know, their baby just had some allergies, and she got some sort of antihistamine at a local clinic. But the way the story is coming out, Ramon, her drug selling boyfriend, is arrested for giving Corina pills. Corina would have had to take those pills. That makes her a willing drug user."

"But what if I can't clear him? Maybe she was."

"Yes, Dan, maybe she was." LaVonne was clearly getting impatient with me. "But that's what they want you to prove wrong, and maybe, with your cop friends, you can clear it up before anyone knows about it. They're not exactly flush with money. You offered to help. At least, that's my best guess to their thinking."

Yesterday I was a nice guy and took a friend to a funeral. Today I feel like I just got caught sharing cigars in the Oval Office. Conflict of interest is something auditors avoid. Doing something to help a friend will get you in trouble every time.

"OK. I'll call them. But I'm gonna need your help too."

"Fair enough. We'll get our butts fired together."

So I did, and the Zavalas and I agreed to meet at Main Place the next day.

Chapter 19

I avoided Marvin's returned call that night. I just let the phone ring. I'd let it wait until after I talked to the Zavalas. He could chew me out later, but at least I would have already met with them.

When I was a kid, I remember one shopping trip where we went to Bullock's in Orange and bought the coming year's school clothing. Back then this mall was an open air thing, with Bullock's on one end, another big chain store on the other that went out of business years ago, along with twenty little shops selling shoes, furniture and hardware placed in between. That was half a century ago, and sometime during that period, someone got the idea to enclose the thing so people could shop there when it rained, without getting wet.

Now, I don't remember rain ever being a real problem here in Orange County, but that was the wisdom of the time, and so Main Place sprang up out of the dust, after years of demolition, redesigns, closings, openings, and design changes.

Main Place mall now sits adjacent to the Santa Ana Freeway, right by a section of it called "The Orange Crush" (so named because traffic really backs up here). It's never been a good arrangement. It got better for a while when they widened the freeway, but it still jams up at rush hour. It was actually fate that situated Main Place here many years ago. Tired of traffic jams, sometimes people exit and go to the mall, until traffic clears up. On Sunday's however, Main Place is a pretty effortless place to get to.

To the south is Santa Ana. To the north is Orange. Neither community could be called a fashion capitol. Nevertheless, Nordstrom, Macy's and J.C Penny are the current mainstays of Main Place, along with a big semicircle food court. LaVonne and I found a table close to the center next to a window, and waited for the Zavala's. It didn't take them long to arrive. It was noisy, so we decided to upgrade to a real restaurant; an Italian place located in the main part of the mall.

"Thank you for taking the time to meet with us," said Luis. Adeline nodded her agreement. "Please... you must think us foolish, but the other day you offered your services..."

I didn't exactly offer services, as I recalled, but I let it slide.

"How can I help?"

"My stepdaughter had this boyfriend. I'm sure you've read in the papers. His name is Ramon Guttierez."

"I understand Guttierez is under arrest from a drug bust," I said.

"I, we... have reasons for wanting Guttierez's arrest to be unfounded." Luis had a hard time saying the name without showing his disdain for the man.

"You don't care for the boy?" I asked.

"I care not at all for him," Luis responded quickly.

Adeline filled in the blanks. "The police think he might have also had something to do with Corina's death." Her eyes welled with tears at the words. "We, uh, know about your previous employment, and we were wondering if you might be able to... check with your friends... and see if it was... you know... true... My daughter was a proponent against drugs. She was constantly rescuing someone..."

It was clear that asking for my help was the hardest thing these people ever had to do in their lives. I turned to Luis. "You said "stepdaughter..."

"Corina was my daughter from a previous marriage," Adeline explained, which now in retrospect, seemed a little obvious, but she went on to tell that when Corina's father, Zacarias Armindarez, abandoned them when Corina was very young, she lost all touch with him. "He never sent child support, and in fact I have no idea where he is now."

Damn. I had fleeting thoughts of Amanda again. I really can't say if she abandoned our marriage or if she was taken, it haunts me like this every day. Something always comes up that reminds me of her mysterious disappearance. I focused my attention on Luis.

"Since Adeline was never able to obtain Armindarez's release, I was unable to adopt Corina as my own," Luis explained further. But I assure you, Corina was my daughter as much as any child could have been."

"I understand. What can you tell me about Guttierez?" The fact that I didn't turn them down right off gave them more hope than they had seen all week.

For the next half hour, the Zavalas told us everything they knew about the young man who sought their daughter's affection. They told us how it was clear he was a dangerous individual, but Corina was a strong-willed girl who only saw the best in people, and therefore allowed him in her otherwise blessed life. But Gutierez had friends, and those friends "hung together" like family, making and getting into all kinds of trouble. You can imagine how much I looked forward to clearing a gang member of murder.

"What can you tell me about the night she died. Do you remember the events?"

"Why do you need to know that?"

"I don't know. Maybe I don't. I just ask questions and try to piece things together. Can you tell me exactly what Corina's movements were that night?"

So the Zavala's together pieced together the events of the evening; how Corina met Theresa after running errands, how she went into the kitchen, how she behaved at the party, when Ramon arrived, when they first noticed she was missing. The whole scene. None of it seemed to shed any light.

Guttierez was currently being held at the Orange County Lockup facility, coincidentally not far from my house, for the drug charge. Police were not anxious to let him go easily, pending their findings at the coroner's office.

"Look," I said. "I am not a cop. A lot of the names and faces have changed since I was on the force. I'll ask a few questions, and see what I can find out. But I just want to prepare you, even if I can find out additional information, you might not get the answer you want to hear."

"Mr. Martyn, please understand," Luis said soberly. "I am a strong proponent for cooperation and good community relations between the police and the Hispanic community, and I know that great strides have been made to improve the police demographic. But the truth is, sometimes, we still do not get straight answers from a county governed by wealthy...."

"...gringos," I finished for him"

Luis flushed. "Well, yes. I suppose that is what I am trying to say."

"That's OK. I understand. Being an ex-cop helps too. I will definitely get a straight answer."

"Exactly."

"Not to worry. Please know I will do my best." And already I felt like a slimy liar because I was not being forthright and revealing the supplier of Corina's allergy medication.

"We have every faith in you."

Chapter 20

I finally called Marvin back when I got home and I think I heard him blow a gasket. "What were you thinking!" he exclaimed more than asked. So I told him, and he told me he'd have to take it to the Vice-Chancellor on Monday.

"Well, Marvin, actually, I don't think that's a good idea yet. After all, what do we really know? The girl got a prescription from one of our Doctors. Lots of people have them. At least let me double-check the records in the morning and confirm that there is no file. Then we'd better let Karen know as well."

Marvin agreed, but told me he'd really rather I not pursue the Guttierez thing, but it was too late. On the way home I had already called my old partner, Steve Partaine, and had asked him if he could ask the coroner a few questions for me. I didn't share that part with Marv.

On Monday morning, I made a certain check in Pediatrics for a file under Corina Zavala's name. I had been right; no file. Not in current records, not in past. We called up files for the past five years. No Corina Zavala, patient. Then I got one of those thoughts that makes you give yourself a forehead slap. "Armindarez. Check for a Corina Armindarez." So poor buggy Rayce had to go back to the archives again, but it still did no good. Even though there was an Armindarez file, it was for a 12 year old boy who had trouble with his tonsils. Definitely not Corina.

Later that morning, I noticed once again that Manuel Maravilla was AWOL. While he had been in most of the morning, he left for a short ten minute break at about ten thirty. It was now eleven thirty and he still hadn't returned.

In the meantime, Steve Partaine gave me a call on my cell phone. "Hey Stretch" (Partaine always thought I needed a nickname. Partaine gives everyone a nickname). "Would you care to join us in a conversation with your favorite neighborhood gang member?"

"Ramon? When?"

"Meet me at OCL at 12:30. We've got a few things to ask Mr. Charm."

Since Orange County Lockup County Facility was close, I'd be able to make the meeting with ease. Normally civies, (civilians like me) are not allowed in questioning sessions, but there are certain rules that get bent among friends, and Steve worked it out so that I was able to be present to provide "advisory information" to him while he and others interviewed Guttierez.

I phoned Marv, updated him on the file situation, and he instructed me to take my next step by questioning Karen. I told him I'd do it right after everyone returned from lunch. I didn't say how I was spending my lunch hour.

Clearance procedures take a bit of time at any jail facility, and OCL is no exception. Soon I was in a room behind a double-glass wall, with my pal Steve.

"OK. Here's what we know. Corina Zavala died of some combination of ingested material. She was evidently taking an antihistamine, maybe some over the counter thing, but the Coroner still hasn't isolated any known "recreational substances" yet. But hell, with the way these kids party with synthetic stuff anymore, hardly a week goes by when some new thing comes out. Yesterday it was Ecstasy, then it was Ecstasy cocktails to offset the overdose side effects. Whatever it was, it isn't FDA approved."

"Zavala's parents say she didn't drug party. In fact, she fought against it."

"Yeah, and my folks told me that reindeer fly too," Steve said. "The truth is, and you know this is true Dan, this crap happens to all kinds of people. Hell, glory boy in there may have slipped it to her without knowing."

I looked up, and a young Latino man had been escorted into the room. He was wearing Musik issue, but he seemed to wear it tougher than the rest of the men in this place. He seemed to really be beyond the room. Investigators asked him questions about what he slipped to Zavala, and his attorney kept repeating instructions to him to keep his mouth shut and citing all kinds of harassment laws against unfounded charges. From my point of view, it looked like the attorney was unnecessary. Ramon Guttierez wasn't about to say anything.

"So what brought him to your doorstep?" I asked.

"We were working a sting in a downtown storefront. We just happened to close the noose on a couple of badass suppliers from Nicaragua the night Ramon here was working his new job. The suppliers had pulled together about sixteen of these wall-sprayers to package product in a warehouse in Anaheim. Ramon was up to his elbows in some very pure cocaine and Saran Wrap. We could forgive the cocaine, but Saran Wrap? That alone should get you twenty."

"Clearly you are an aluminum foil guy."

"No. I like straws from Mickey D's. That way, you get the whole kit; drug and inhaler in one tidy package."

"You're nothing, if not efficient."

I looked at Guttierez through the glass.

"It doesn't figure."

"What do you mean? We caught the kid red-handed. Of course he's a drug supplier."

"Steve, you just described to me a stupid kid who got caught packaging stuff for someone else, hoping to gain status among peers and spending cash. But he's not the distribution end. He was involved in a cocaine business. But you yourself said the stuff that killed Corina wasn't main line stuff."

"So, he diversifies on the side."

"Yeah, and I'm sure his Nicaraguan employers encouraged him to open up his own franchise with another supplier. Do you have anything, anywhere, that links Ramon to the kind of Rave drugs you think killed Corina?"

Partaine looked at me dumbly. "What. Are you trying to clear this clown of murder?"

"Just stating the obvious. You've got a case against a kid who was stupid enough to get his nose in the middle of something bigger than he could handle. He was packaging cocaine. Take it, and run with it. In my book, that's plenty of crime for one week. But the Zavala question is remote at best. What have you got, really? You don't even know what killed her. You're only going to screw around here until you foul up the good charge you have in the bag. In the mean time, you could wreck the reputation of one kid who happened to be one of the few straight arrows we'd like to see more of. Is that the kind of police work we do now?"

Partaine rubbed the back of his red neck, and ran his hand over his close cropped hair. Every hair stood firmly in it's hedgehog place. I'd never noticed before how much Steve looked like a cross between the Southern Cop in those James Bond movies and a member of a rock band. A weird and wonderful marriage to be sure.

We watched the grilling for a couple more minutes. It was useless. At one point, I swore Ramon looked straight at me, but then I had enough experience to know he was "psyching" the window. He couldn't see me, but in case the glass was hiding some unknown witness, prisoners often picked a spot on the window, about eye-height, on the chance they could frighten the potential witness to silence. Ramon clearly knew all the tricks, and there was no breaking him.

Steve knew they weren't going to get anything.

"Wanna ask him anything?"

"Sure," I said.

We went together around to the other door, and Steve pointed to me and said to the guard "He's with me." More and more I felt like I was with a rock star. I was going backstage.

As we entered, another cop gave us the "who the hell is this" look, and Partaine ignored him. I was focused on Ramon. The light was stark, and the room smelled of sweat. I took a seat next to Partaine on the other side of the table.

Ramon looked at me and said "Who are you?"

Partaine said "Look twerp, we're already set to charge you with possession, and various other lovely little transgressions related to this mess you got yourself in. This guy wanted to see you about something else. Just answer his questions."

Ramon tilted his head and sneered at me. "Shit. You toros gonna trump me up on some other shit, ain'tcha."

Actually, no," I said, and just sat for a second. "I'm not a cop. I might actually be the closest thing you have to a friend within five blocks."

Ramon's snaky eyes narrowed. "Give me one good reason I should talk to you, Puto."

Not a nice word. My proctologist knows it well. How Corina got mixed up with this little sack of hate, I couldn't imagine.

"OK. Try this. Corina Zavala."

In one split second, the tough little turd turned to mush. His eyes went from hate to tears, his mood went from rage to despair. He let out another curse word, this one not directed at me, but it seemed to the air above. After a while, he calmed a bit, so I asked.

"I need you to tell me if you gave her anything that might have killed her."

"Are you crazy? I loved Corina. I wouldn't hurt her."

"Maybe so, but you obviously aren't the clearest thinker I have ever met, and I never met a tweaker that thought twice about sharing their joy."

"Hey!" He said, the anger back. "I ain't no goddam tweaker. That crank shit is for idiots."

Then he softened again.

"OK, ok, I am obviously going down for something. But not Corina. I swear to God don't know what happened to her."

"When did you last see her?"

"I been." and he looked to Partaine. "Busy. I hadn't seen her for days. I went to the party late, she was dead."

And the word "Dead" set him off again in anguish.

Crap. Having someone like Guttierez look you in the eye and deny something isn't exactly proof of anything, and the last thing you should ever do is believe the word of a criminal. But there was something in the way he said this that sold it. Sometimes, when certain things matter to an individual, they suddenly summon the ability in them to convince you they are being the truth. If you could bottle it, you could help millions of people fake sincerity and get away with it.

Guttierez was clearly telling me the truth. I was sure of it.

I waited again. Partaine fidgeted.

"Can you give me anything at all."

But Guttierez was no good to anyone anymore. I wasn't going to get anything helpful here. It was time to go.

Partaine said to no one in particular, "Forget it." Turning to the guard, he said "Pull him out of here, Junior, We'll just go with what we've got." Another nickname. Sort of a default one. Anyone under 35, Steve calls "Junior."

Sometimes, when a cop knows someone is guilty of a crime, but can't produce hard evidence, you get anxious and antsy, overstepping rules, hoping to produce something prosecutable. That's the kind of police work that beats the shit out of justice, and that's when mistakes happen. If you are a lucky cop, you'll keep friends around you who can keep you focused on doing things right, without cutting corners. Steve and I had that kind of relationship. The LA cops at Rampart division did not have that kind of support, and that's what led to the big Rampart scandal.

Orange County has its own share of corruption. The Sheriff himself had been drummed out of office for selling badges to political supporters, and barely escaped with some minor charges. He was probably guilty of a lot more, but no one was able to convince everyone on his jury. It just happened to work in my favor that some of the rule bending still existed, and bent my way, allowing me in.

Partaine was hoping I would have knocked the wind out of Guttierez, and given him more. Not being on the force, I might have been able to curb Steve's zeal earlier. There was no doubt about it.

But Guttierez was guilty of playing a packaging role in a coke operation, and now Partaine was going to give it to the prosecutor.

Steve looked at me. "You're a real pain in the ass. I don't have any idea why I bothered to try to help you."

"Funny. I was just about to say the same thing about you. But thanks."

"The sign on the door says it all," he said.

I glanced at the sheriff department logo. "Protect and Serve."

Chapter 21

I knocked on Karen's door.

"Come in Dan."

Ooo. Psychic. I like that in a girl.

I took a seat opposite Karen in the chair farthest from the door. LaVonne Fontaine followed me and took the other one.

"So, what's my favorite auditor found so far," beamed Karen. She was looking right at me and I loved the "favorite auditor" stuff. If you ever get audited and look like a million dollars, always try buttering up the auditor. We're supposed to be impervious to that stuff, but dang if it sometimes doesn't charm the socks off of us.

Then again, I suppose it didn't sit as well with LaVonne. In fact, it was if LaVonne wasn't in the room at all. Karen looked at me, and I looked back, and it was about one tenth of a second of pure lust flying across the desk in both directions. It was the best tenth of a second, because for just that bit of time, I totally forgot that Karen Taylor's office was in deep trouble.

"Well." I started. I didn't want to go on, but forward man, forward.

"If everything was perfect, you'd think we were terrible auditors."

"Uh Oh." Karen said. "Sometimes, I think I'd like some terrible auditors. What's wrong."

"Actually," LaVonne butted in, just to assert herself into the meeting, "You've got a lot of stuff going right."

Karen did a take, as if she was surprised LaVonne was even in the room, and then turned it into a "Oh. Well, that sounds good" type of expression.

"Yes, it's true," I continued. Over the past week, LaVonne and I have reviewed eight of the main business functions here, and most of them have turned out most satisfactory. Your insurance billings are accurate, and you're collection ratio is one of the highest we've encountered this year. But we have discovered some other things that could be pretty significant."

I wanted to downplay it. No sense inciting panic, when we don't even know if panic is warranted. It's kind of like yelling "Movie!" in a Firehouse, or something like that.

Of course, you can argue that if Karen was some horrible little troll of a person, my approach would have been totally different. All I can say now, in retrospect, is "Guilty as charged."

"When was the last time you reviewed your prescription records?" I found myself asking.

Karen took an immediate cool. "You were looking at patient prescriptions?"

"Not exactly," said LaVonne. "No, we weren't reviewing private records. I just did a review of your pad records, and discovered that a couple of pads are unaccounted for."

"Criminy, LaVonne," Karen said (yes, I know, but believe it or not, she really did say 'criminy'). "Most places don't even keep duplicate, numeric pads. If I didn't have them, you wouldn't even have looked at it."

"Yeah, I know Karen," I cut in. "But since you had the control, we happened to look at it, and discovered a problem. Now, maybe in another consulting session, we can discuss the necessity for the control, but since it's in place, we thought you'd like to know. You can always include comments in your response letter to our audit."

"'How bad is it?"

"Well, in light of some other things that have come up in the past week, it might have a pretty high significance."

Karen let that soak in for a minute.

"What other things."

I took a deep breath. "Karen," I began. "Have you ever heard of a patient by the name of Corina Zavala, or Corina Armindarez?"

Karen's perfect little eyebrows furrowed. "Well, no, but then again, I don't really get to know the names of all our patients. But..."

"Yes..." I said, encouragingly.

"Isn't Zavala the name of that girl on the news?"

Ooo. Two! She is savvy with current events. A plus for the beautiful woman behind and below the glass desk.

"Yep," I said, and I really didn't know how to put it gently. "You see, we seem to have stumbled across what

Could be a major PR problem, if not criminal. It seems that we may be somehow connected to her death."

You could have knocked Karen over with a shrimp.

"What. How? Who else knows about this?"

So I told her how LaVonne had been her neighbor, and how we had been invited to the funeral, and how I had found a prescription bottle in the Zavala home for an antihistamine with Dr. Bolo's name on it. I showed her the prescription information, and how we couldn't locate any record of Zavala in any of the clinic's files, and how some other files had been missing for a day but reappeared later. I decided it was probably better at this time to NOT tell her about messing with Scott Thomason at the funeral, or meeting with the Zavalas, or going over to the Musik jail to watch the police put the screw to Ramon Guttierez. This is what we call in the University Administration business as "eight kinds of stupid."

"So what do we do now?" said a stunned Karen.

"I'd suggest you and Connie review the records yourselves. See if you come up with answers. Maybe there's something we're missing. After all, we may just be looking at an error... a very visible error... where we made a legitimate health decision for a young lady with allergies and she mixed things up for herself. But better we find out about it before anybody else does."

"Anything else?" asked a weary Karen Taylor.

"Well, um. Yes."

"What."

"Do you have any idea where Manuel Maravilla is right now?"

Chapter 22

I would like to report that for the next sixteen hours, nothing changed. No incredible coincidence occurred that led to a new problem; no stunning conversation occurred that gave me reason to report you in snappy banter what a clever conversationalist I am. I just drove home, and happened to drive by the guy with signs by Santa Ana College, but to be quite honest, I don't have any recollection about what the sign said. Even that was a bust. Let's face it; I'm writing this several months after the fact and quite frankly, I doubt if I am catching the actual conversations word for word. If I had that kind of memory, I could rent myself out as a court reporter or something. No, what you are getting here is the truth, as near as I can recall it, and unfortunately, I don't recall a damn thing happening the night after I told Karen Taylor her department was falling apart.

It always amuses me how some book detectives can remember exactly what they had for dinner that night, or what they were wearing. Spenser is always describing his clothing or worse yet, his buddy Hawk's outfit, as if anyone cared, and Matthew Scudder can give you complete menus at any given moment. What's wrong with these guys? I can barely remember what I had for breakfast this morning. Well, OK, it was a bear claw from Starbucks with a cup of traditional roast, but as my father would have said, who gives a fat rat's ass?

I could make it up, but then I'd really be jeopardizing my credibility, wouldn't I? I'm sure you realize that if circumstances occurred that really made me look like a complete jackass, I probably wouldn't tell you the whole story. If something happened that was embarrassing, and did have pertinence to the story, you know I'd probably just gussy it up. I doubt very seriously if you'd even mind. There's nothing worse than a guy who writes a book about himself and then makes himself look like a complete fool. You and I both know someone like that would need weeks and weeks of therapy.

Anyway, nothing happened, so I went home and put on my blue lounging pajamas and sheepskin slippers and poured myself a Jack Daniels, two fingers worth, and sat back reading the latest issue of Maxim Magazine (an photo article about some bad actress I never heard of). Later, I made myself a wonderful dinner of fried scallops, sautéed in butter and shallots, and watched 22 minutes of Jeopardy. I was up to $16,000 before I asked for a lifeline, and then realizing that was a different game, I fell asleep listening to Bill Charlap jazz trio CD. And not once all evening did I do anything stupid... as near as I can recall.

Chapter 23

Amanda used to always say to me that if wishes were horses, beggars would ride, and I confess I always had a hard time figuring out what the heck that meant. Oh, I understand the proverb; beggars wish for everything they get, so they'd have a plethora of ponies. I just always wondered how that applied to the facts at hand whenever Amanda brought it up. I'd be pondering my fate as a permanently though only slightly disabled cop, and she'd bring up the riding beggars. I didn't see the relation. Maybe she had some sort of wish herself; to ride away from her troubles.

Anyway, the next morning, I saw my beggar... the guy with the signs. I wondered for a moment if he had a gaggle of horses. He was still on his watch on the corner of Bristol and 17th, an area of town renown for its lack of equine transportation. Today his sign said:

"Parents; the sage says:
Do you know where
your ethics are?"

Maybe I've lived alone so long now that this stuff makes sense to me. The world has become a more dangerous place, with parents yielding to the call of biological and hormonal urges, but disinterested in actually taking on the role of parents. For that reason, I felt especially sad for the Zavalas; here were clearly two parents who did their duty and embraced their roles as parents wholeheartedly. To lose the product of such a good home makes the Corina tragedy especially sorrowful. As involved in their daughter's upbringing as they were, they still lost her. Meanwhile, the streets and malls are filled with skanky kids who's parents wrote them off years ago, and yet they get to live.

There is a shopping center on the corner opposite my beggar, and by coincidence, it was the location of the Drug-co Pharmacy Corina used to have her prescription filled. It was one of those 24 hour locations, and since it wasn't in the best area of town, it was designed to be a little less easier to get into and out of than a pharmacy in, say; Newport Beach. Just inside the door, there were racks with advertising flyers highlighting Drug-co's specials of the week, and some "Apartment finder" books. A chrome entry gate counted me as I went through the turnstile, and I made my way to the back of the store where the pharmacy was located. A fat kid, about nine years old, was checking out the condom rack. Always look for good recreation on your way to school.

The set-up seemed a little crowded. The pea-soup colored Formica counter was angled at 45 degrees, allowing for an area for customers to wait while the pharmacist filled out your prescription. No one was visible at this early hour, so I dinged the bell on the counter. A small oriental woman came out from behind the stocking shelves in the glassed off area, clearly irritated that I dared to use the bell. I introduced myself.

"Good morning. I'm Dan Martyn, and I was wondering if you could help me by answering a few questions."

Obviously, she was wary of me, because anything out of the ordinary, in this area of town, at this early hour, would always be suspect. She eyed me suspiciously, so I forged ahead, as if what I was doing was perfectly normal.

I told her where I worked, and explained to her that I was doing an audit of one of our departments. I gave her one of my impressive business cards.

She took the card with both hands, and studied it as if it were a subpoena. I told you they were impressive.

"We're doing a simple audit of prescriptions written by our Pediatrics department, and in a random sample, we pulled a prescription that was apparently filled here." I didn't explain how "we" came to that conclusion. I just thought I'd glide right through that part.

"What we are doing is ensuring that the prescriptions written are filled consistent with our records, and so that leads me to you. I'm sure you get this all the time." I was sure she was never faced with this question before in her life. I stopped talking.

She just looked at me with a blank stare. I knew I had her. The first person who says a word, loses.

"Well, um... what do you need?"

"Not much," I smiled. "I just have this one prescription to verify. It was written to a Ms. C. Zavala, and was filled by this Pharmacy sometime earlier this month. Do you have a record of it?"

"Those records are confidential," she said.

Uh-oh.

"Of course," I quickly replied. "That's why I'm here. We're not asking you to provide us with any confidential information. Only to confirm the information I already have. In fact, we'd be concerned if you did volunteer any information. No basically, we're just asking if you can confirm the information we have already."

I forged ahead.

"Your records indicate that a prescription was written, signed by Dr. Adam Bolo, for 30 capsules Zantac, 20mg's. to be taken once a day. It was filled at this pharmacy on June 7. We'd be appreciative if you could just confirm those facts."

"Well, sure... I think I can do that."

She went back into the glass room, and flipped on the monitor on a computer system. The greenish glow cast a strange image in her aluminum-framed glasses. In a few minutes, she came back.

"All that information is exactly true. Do you want to see a copy of the prescription?"

If wishes were horses.....

In a few minutes, she produced the prescription form that had Dr. Bolo's signature. It was indeed a Pediatrics prescription form, and it was numbered "4759." This was far more than I hoped for, and I wanted to skedaddle out of there before her supervisor came back and threw something at me.

Then another question occurred to me.

"Thanks," I said. "One more thing. Can you tell me how many prescriptions you have filled written by um... (and I looked at the prescription as if I was just trying to recall) Dr. Bolo.

"Sure," she said. She was comfortable with me by now. "I can pull it up on our computers. Let's see... "and she typed a couple of strokes into the computer. "Twenty-seven in the past month... and..." She proceeded to give me numbers. Big ones. I struggled to hide my surprise.

Dr. Bolo had definitely written Corina Zavala's prescription, and we had no record of it. But even more disturbing, somehow, a bunch of other prescriptions had managed to get filled in this same damn pharmacy, which isn't exactly near our Medical Center. Far more than is statistically predictable. Somehow, this Pharmacy was tied into the mystery. But I had no idea how. I only knew our problem just grew exponentially.

Physicians, the Sage says:
"Do you know where your
Prescriptions are?"

Chapter 24

Bristol is just a few streets over from the street where the Medical Center, And just one main street over from Grand, where the Gazette has it's large headquarters. I wasn't really thinking much about the Gazette when I stopped on the way to Pediatrics at a Starbucks on the way. I ordered a large coffee, and I hope you know me well enough by now to know I am not one of those people who will use the word "Venti" for large. Nor do I order fluffed up foamed doodads with Italian sounding but definitely not Italian names.

LaVonne, on the other hand, orders a "Venti, Skinny Hazelnut Latte," and even though I find it embarrassing to order it, I got her one to take to the office for her. The "Barrista" (Italian again), a rather dull looking boy with a pierced lip, burn on his neck, and bright purple hair, placed the order without batting an eye. I don't know. Maybe they were stapled or something. He definitely didn't look as awake as his eyes were.

They called my name, and I picked up LaVonne's drink, turned, and darn near bumped into Thomason. Clearly coming to this Starbucks was a really dumb idea.

"Martyn! You Rat Bastard!"

"Hi Scott." I am a very friendly fellow.

I tried to make it a casual bump in, sidesaddle out the door type of exit, but too late. Thomason was on my tail.

"Martyn, you owe me."

Now that I knew what I knew about the Bolo prescriptions, I really didn't want to talk to him. This was the very last place I wanted to be, cornered with the very last person I wanted to be cornered with.

"Hey, Scotty, I am sorry I messed with your brain the other day. I was just having a little fun. I really was just at the church with my friend. You know how it is."

I was appealing to his sense of humanity. Evidently reporters don't have a sense of humanity.

"Danny boy, if I find out you are hiding something from me, I swear I am gonna."

"What, Scott. What are you gonna do to me?"

The kid sputtered a bit, but he knew he was grasping at what he really thought were empty threats. If he only really knew the potential that kidnapping and torturing me could hold, he probably would be putting a bag over my head right now.

"What are you doing in this part of town?

Oh jeez.

"Scott. I live in Irvine. I took surface streets this way on my way to the Med Center. No reason. I just was dodging traffic on the freeway."

He looked crestfallen. His last hope was met and vanquished. Ace reporter.

I turned my back on him and got in my car. I left him staring at the back end of my car as I drove out of the parking lot.

When I got back to the Pediatrics, I found LaVonne, who was happy that I brought her the "skinny" latte. "No Sugar, Non-fat. Just the way you like it." She grinned and savored it. LaVonne loves her lattes.

Someone was touching up the paint on the elephants. No warm and fuzzy Babar-type elephants here: These were very realistic looking African elephants. I remember thinking; Dumbo's mother was an Indian elephant, but Dumbo's oversized ears shaped like these African elephants. Disney was clearly a pioneer in cross-cultural marriages. Was Dumbo really intended to be an allegory for racial unity?

Then I looked at the rest of the paintings. Circuses are filled with scary stuff. Lions. Clowns. My sister took her daughter to the circus once, and they had a guy who wrestled alligators. Though her seats were at the top of the grandstands, one of the alligators got out of the center ring, and my nephew freaked out. He was sure he was going to be alligator meat.

I had a feeling that if Marvin found out what I had just done at Drug-co, I'd be alligator meat too. Even worse that I was having coffee encounters with Thomason. My cop background just hates loose ends. Usually, you never hit a home run by getting more information, but occasionally, you can finesse a good fact or two out of a hostile witness.

LaVonne was already reviewing prescription pads. They came in pads of 50. I gave her the number we were looking for, but the pad numbered 4750-4799 was nowhere in sight. Several other series were missing too.

I made an appointment to talk with Adam Bolo. He had a morning in surgery, and of course, after a morning of stressful surgery, saving lives of small children, nothing relaxes you more than a nice chat with an auditor. He was, well, a hairy man. His hair seemed to have a mind of its own: While he still had plenty, it was fine and scraggly. His beard was equally fuzzy. He looked like the prospector guy in the Rudolph the Red-nosed Reindeer. You know the one: the claymation movie they show every year where Rudolph, the prospector, and an elf manage to yank out all of the abominable snowman's teeth. Give Bolo a knit cap and a plaid shirt, and I bet he could find gold by tasting his pick.

Of course, there are never any easy explanations for anything. Bolo was a surgeon, and didn't really have many allergy patients. Certainly not Corina Zavala, under any version of her name. He could not recall seeing the young lady, and he prided himself on his ability to remember all his patients. Adam Bolo was either an elaborate liar covering up the fact he forgot to record a prescription, or he really never saw Corina.

"Can I ask you one more thing?" I ventured. "Any idea why so many of your prescriptions would be filled at a certain pharmacy in Santa Ana?"

Yukon Cornelius did that thing you do with your head when surprised. His eyes got big and his head perked up. This was clearly news to him.

So the mystery was still unsolved, and I was running out of ideas. As an auditor, my job is to run tests, verify information, and write a report. I was going to have to put aside my sleuthing. I must have been getting rusty. Officially, all I had discovered was that a prescription was written for a girl and we couldn't find any record of it. Unofficially, I knew a whole bunch more prescriptions were probably being filled too. Had I been a cop, I probably could have found out a whole bunch more information at the pharmacy. But this was getting really bad.

Our prescription pads were walking out of here, and Dr. Bolo was getting set-up for one helluva problem.

Chapter 25

That night at home I accessed my calendar from work via the web: one of the advantages for working for the University. I had forgotten that I was to testify the next morning in court regarding a fraud case I had discovered last winter.

My testimony was pretty cut and dried. I didn't really have to review anything prior to the court proceeding. I was familiar with the case and I had done this scores of times, not only as a police officer, but as an auditor. You'd be surprised to learn how often University auditors are called to testify. The duty was easy, and I had no problem with either attorney. I just find them amusing.

Contrary to popular belief, not all attorneys are horses hind ends. Occasionally, you get other pieces of the horse's anatomy as well. This case was about a kid who had been let go as a student employee because they caught him submitting bogus petty cash receipts to the University's

Cashier for reimbursement on a regular basis. I discovered it in a routine audit when I noticed the payments. His boss confronted him, he did a worm in his shorts, and ran out the door. The University's Risk Management team decided to prosecute.

Once my testimony was done, I got cross examined, but you could tell the kid's attorney was new at this. I found myself wanting to help him, but I just stuck to the facts. That's usually a good rule of thumb. Never lie under oath. I hand out these tips for free.

Free to go, still under oath, and hungry, I left the courtroom to get a sandwich. Outside the Santa Ana courtroom is my old pal Vic. Vic sells Saran wrapped sandwiches for a couple of bucks, and Fanta beverages from a little stand on wheels. Nothing looked good, so I just asked for an orange soda.

"Whoa, Dan Martyn!" said Vic. "I hear you making gangsta pals."

Nothing gets by Vic. His ear is tuned to the street like a violin. Or something. The analogy sucks.

"Yeah? What did you hear?"

"Word is you are smelling around Guttierez ass to see if the paper sticks. Makin' the Bones kinda nervous," he added under his breath as he discretely handed me an Orange Fanta.

Colorful street vendors amuse me.

"Yeah? The Bones?"

"You didn't hear nuttin' from me," he said, as his attention turned to a pretty brown haired attorney in a dark brown business suit. The uniform of Attorneyship looked especially good on her shapely figure.

I have known Vic the Stick for over twenty years, and I know when he is done sharing his information. I paid with a twenty and walked away without change. $20 is a lot of money for a soft drink, and a lousy tip for the information he gave, but Vic is always happy for anything. He works cheap, and frequently, and knows something for everyone. I wouldn't be surprised if the attorney was getting input on her case as well. I walked away, a bit disconcerted, but informed.

The Bones are a Santa Ana street gang with a nasty reputation. To hear I am making them nervous probably isn't the best news one can hear.

I had been dismissed from the courtroom, so I knew I could go on my way back to work, but work wasn't exactly what I had in mind. Without the need to call Marvin, they could assume I was at the courthouse all day. So I decided to make one other stop that afternoon, Fanta in hand.

There are two malls near the Courthouse. The first is called The Block, and it's nearby. The second one was Main Place, where LaVonne and I had met the Zavalas.

It seems I always needed shoes, a curse that would follow me all my life. It seems my shoes are always in disrepair. It was bad enough with two good legs. When I wound up with a bum leg, the wear and tear on the left shoe always seemed to be greater than my right.

I decided to head up to Main Place to update my foot wardrobe. The Block was a better choice, I reasoned, because every other store there is a shoe store. But I prefer the stodgier old Main Place mall over the newer and trendier Block, because I prefer shoes like Florsheim over some shoe named after a marsupial.

Turns out I wasn't the only one playing hooky. I parked the car, and who should I park six spaces over from, but LaVonne. I recognized her car by the opossum University mascot sticker in the back window. Southern California is up to its butt in opossums. In the sixties, when the University was established, students flexing their rebellious muscles thought it would be a bit of a joke to vote the opossum as the mascot of our university.

It was actually not a bad choice though. Turns out that even though opossums are dense, somewhat stupid creatures (look it up), they can, if under attack, strike a rather hideous, menacing pose. right before they try to play dead. If looks could kill, the face of a vicious opossum is an fearsome sight to behold; Perfect to adorn a University sweatshirt, or the aforementioned window sticker.

I knew it was LaVonne's car because her son put it in the window for her, and we have already addressed his skills previously. It was somewhat askew, had bubbles trapped in it, and made LaVonne's car drop about $2000 in value the minute he affixed to the window. I recognized it instantly.

I stepped into Nordstrom, the store adjoining the parking lot, and there she was, looking at some sort of girlish decorative item in the area just inside the door. When she saw me, she just about fainted.

"Oh crap. You caught me. Super sleuth. How in God's name did you track me down here?"

"I have my mysterious ways," I countered, not about to tell her it was a total fluke. I took my cue. "Does Marvin know you are taking a shopping break?" I said in my most judgmental voice.

"Lord no, and don't you tell him." She snapped.

"OK. I will keep your discretion a secret, if you keep quiet about me going to buy some shoes."

Nordstrom has lots of good brand men's shoes, but I shopped there once and the manager talked to me like I was 100 years old. He treated me like an invalid, and while I do admit to a gimp leg, I thought he was being far too condescending. No more Nordstrom shoes for me, said I.

We walked through Nordy's, and LaVonne went to the right to hit a health food store. I went left, and took the elevator down and walked down toward the center. Down by The Limited, there's a little hole-in-the-wall shoe store that sells, believe it or not, shoes without three-inch platforms.

I was able to get a decent pair of black Florsheim loafers, sans tassles, at a fairly reasonable price. I bought them, put them on, and slip-slided over to the trash bin to dump my old ones. Yes, I could have given them to the Salvation Army, but because they were so shot, they'd probably end up doing the same thing.

I returned to the end of the mall where I had parted ways with LaVonne, and trudged up the stairs, scraping the bottom of my shoes against the non-slip strips in order to give my new soles some traction. LaVonne was still in the Health Food store, engaged in conversation with a young lady who looked familiar.

LaVonne finished her purchase of Adkins bars (she's always trying fad diets), and then we walked over to the food court to grab some lunch. Finally, some food!

To save time, we both went to Ruby's for a burger and vanilla Coke, (LaVonne's was a diet) and I chowed-down on some French Fries. My arteries hate me.

"Who was that girl at the store? I thought I had seen her somewhere before."

"You did. Her name is Theresa, and she's a little young for you, hound dog."

"I don't want her body. I just wondered where I've seen her"

"Probably at the Zavalas. She was a friend of Corina's." I made a mental note.

"So what did you buy?"

"Oh, stuff for another stupid diet. I was thinking of doing that Protein/No carb diet everyone's doing."

"Be careful with that," I cautioned. "A girl needs her carbs. More than that, you need grains and roughage."

"Well, aren't you the health care expert."

"Didn't you hear? I've recently decided to work under a certain manager in Pediatrics."

That caught LaVonne so off guard that Diet Vanilla Coke came out her nose.

"Aaagh! I hate it when that happens!"

"No, seriously, there are two things you must never do. Cut grains and snort coke... even if it is vanilla."

"Well, as for the roughage, Theresa suggested that if I do this diet, I should take this supplement. You know, it feels good to see that kid doing well in her job... finally.

"Has she been a problem?"

"Well, I don't know about employment, but her life has been topsy-turvy. Since she started here, she seems to have taken a liking to it."

"Sounds like she has your health needs well in hand."

"I'll start the diet tomorrow but who can pass up a Ruby's Beach Burger?" LaVonne explained, as she polished off her lunch. Those of us locals know that even though the Beach Burger is no longer on the menu, you can still ask for it, and they will make it for you. Same for their knackwurst burger, the Ruby Dog.

I knew better than to continue a conversation about diets with LaVonne. Actually, weight has never been a problem of mine, but probably because of my swimming. LaVonne, on the other hand, while an attractive woman, is always waging war in the battle of the bulge. Frankly, I like LaVonne just the way she is, but our culture seems to have everyone in a sense of guilt over any figure that doesn't look Hollywood perfect.

It strikes me as odd, because, as I looked around the mall, Hundreds of people seemed to be carrying extra baggage, a few were downright skinny, and Hollywood perfection was rarer still. Granted, eating healthier is a good thing, but everyone seems to go crazy when food comes up... er... not that food coming up is the image I meant to describe. I meant the subject of food.

We quickly finish lunch and headed back to Pediatrics.

Chapter 26

We got back around 2:00, and after our shopping spree, I figured I'd better check in with Marvin. Even Marvin wouldn't believe that I would be tied up the entire day at the courthouse. I called him to update him about my testimony, blah blah blah, ok, fine. any messages?

"Oh yeah," Martin said. "Your old cop buddy, Partaine called."

I called him back.

"Hey Stretch. 'Thought I'd give you a heads up. Your boy just got released."

"My boy?"

"Sure. You know. Guttierez. Rah-Moan. Your tweaker supplier just got released on a technicality."

"What kind of technicality?"

"Seems our raid of their facility was bogus. A screw-up with warrants. We managed to salvage the big fish, but the packagers are getting off easy. Guttierez is one free jerk-off."

"Anyone else know about this?"

"Pretty soon everyone will know, Stretch. Your favorite reporter was here when he walked out of Musik."

"Lemme guess. Thomason?"

"Yep. Seems this guy has a bug up his butt about this Zavala girl. Convinced that there's more to the girl's death than reported. Someone tipped him off that Guttierez was temporarily sleeping over at our place, and so newshound has been here waiting. So the next question begs to be asked."

I should have seen it coming.

"What's the University's interest in this thing, Stretch?"

I assured Steve that I was only asking about Guttierez as a favor for LaVonne's neighbors, and that was it, but I could tell Partaine wasn't buying it. I could tell by the way he said "Uh-huh" in response.

"You will keep me posted if anything comes up, right Stretch?"

"Really Steve. There's no problem. The parents asked me to look into Ramon to see if I could clear him. Now I can take the credit, and they will love me." I half-lied by telling the truth, but I've gotten really good at justifying my lies. My dad was the only one who ever caught me. Partaine was close, but gave me the benefit of the doubt.

Partaine wanted to know if there was anything about Guttierez he should know about. Technically, I had no connection to him with what I had found, although I did know someone was out there waltzing around writing prescriptions on our pads. And Guttierez's friends evidently heard that I was asking him some questions.

It all kind of made sense now. Who else but Ramon would have told them? But was it fair to suggest anything other than what Partaine knew about Guttierez? Absolutely not. I had no reason to make a connection between Guttierez and Corina's demise. And as much as I hated it, I believed Ramon.

About four o'clock, Manuel strolled by the front desk, pockets filled with a Hershey bars and pens, and stepped out the front door. I glanced at LaVonne. She understood, and nodded. I followed Manuel.

Understand, normally audits don't include tails. But by now, LaVonne knew I missed my police work enough that if I could possibly find a reason to act like a cop, I would. Maravilla's missing time was a concern. With all the loose ends hanging, I figured if I grabbed one and held on it might lead to something.

I used to be really good at a follow. I still think I am, but every now and then, my knee tells me I'm wrong. The idea is to not be noticed. Limping guys are usually easily to spot. However, if your mark has no reason to think he's being followed, he usually won't be looking for a tail. Manuel had no reason. He was simply doing what he did several times a week; disappearing off of the time clock.

I followed him to radiology. I couldn't go inside, because there was nowhere to hide, so I sat down in a visitor chair way down the hall and read about Brittany Spears changing her clean-cut image. I thought the magazine was old, but it was new. Oops, she did it again.

Then, Manuel came out of radiology and took an immediate left. By the time I got to the hall, I couldn't see him, but I noticed the door to the stairway half-way down the hall was just latching. I entered carefully, and listened as some male shoes shuffled above. He was two flights above me, and exited the stairwell on the fourth floor. I sprinted as quickly as possible up the stairs, and opened the door quietly about two inches.

Manuel was standing at a nurse's station, and was laughing and passing out Hershey bars to two nurses, who in turn, handed him a clip board. He reviewed something, thanked them, and then walked over to the elevator. He got in.

Damn. Tails in an elevator suck.

There had been three other people in the elevator, and it stopped on every floor on the way down. Manual could have gotten off on any one of them. I turned and went back down the stairs to the ground floor. As I came out of the stairwell, I damn near ran into him, but he didn't notice me. He had just passed the stairwell, and was engaged in a animated discussion with a young intern.

Together they exited the building, Manuel went left, the intern went right. Alone again, I followed him to the parking lot. My car was on the fourth level, and I had no idea where he was parked, but on instinct I went straight to my car. I got in and drove down the levels as quickly as possible to the exit. Sure enough, as I rounded a corner, I spotted Manual in a grey ten-year old Toyota Celica, about four cars ahead of me. Perfect.

I saw him leave the parking structure to the left, but the car in front of me had to stop at the booth to pay the attendant. Apparently the lady didn't think about it until she actually got to the gate, and there was a slight delay as she fumbled for her purse, found money, and cleared by the gate. The attendant waived me through, eyeing my parking permit, and I turned left.

Manuel was nowhere to be seen, but all was not lost. The parking structure was located off the main street, so you had to drive about 15 miles per hour around the pretty new Medical Center complex to get to the main exit. I drove 20. Sure enough, Manuel was just clearing the green light, and turned right just as the light was changing. I got to the corner, and watched as he made another right on Chapman Avenue.

I followed him through some new construction, and on the far side of the 57 freeway, he turned right again. This was a residential street, mixed with a few businesses. We passed the Turnip Rose, a restaurant I've been to frequently because the Institute of Internal Auditors often have regional meetings there. Actually, it's not exactly a restaurant; more a meeting facility, but who cares right now, I'm on a tail.

After a few complicated turns and twists, Manuel was in downtown Santa Ana, and he pulled up in front of single story white building with white painted windows. We were about a block and a half away from the Drug-co Pharmacy I had been to earlier in the week. I pulled over a block behind him, and waited until he entered before I went any further.

He entered the building, and so I was able to merge back into traffic and drive by the building. It was in disrepair, but had a plastic sign hanging over the door that simply said the word "Clinica." As I drove by, a young latina woman was exiting the building with two small children in tow.

So now I knew where Manuel was disappearing to, but I was uncertain what it meant. I did have an idea... but I had to be sure.

Chapter 27

I pulled into an open parking space about two blocks away, and walked back to the Clinic. It was in a fairly run-down building, and the glass in the front door had a slight crack in the corner. The door handled was weathered and felt rough to my hand as I entered. It was surprising to note how clean the interior was compared to the outside of the building. The walls were painted with a fresh coat of gloss white, and there were scenic pictures on the wall, as if they had been taken from the National Geographic, only larger.

Directly in front of me as I entered was a reception desk, staffed by two very busy women. One was on the phone, speaking Spanish to someone who evidently wanted to change an appointment. The second woman had her nose buried in her filing and didn't look up when I entered. The woman on the phone gave me a sideways glance, and then another one, this time taking her pen and tapping sideways on a clipboard that was sitting on the counter between us. It was a patient sign-in sheet, so I took it and began filling it out. There were three columns; for my name, the doctor I was here to see (I put MR. Maravilla), and a place to check if I was a new patient. Patient wasn't exactly what I was, so I left it blank.

I returned the clipboard to the desk, and the lady on the phone scrutinized it absently as she completed her call. Now she looked closer at my sign-in sheet and gave me a more appraising look. "You're here to see Dr. Maravilla?" she quizzed, as if I had no business being there.

"Is Maravilla the doctor who is in?" I asked, as if my question was an answer to her question.

"Dr. Maravilla is a very busy man." She replied indignantly.

"You have no idea," I murmured, more to myself than to her.

She looked at me with one eyebrow raised. She reminded me of the WWF wrestler the Rock... not just because of the eyebrow.

"I'm an Auditor." I said.

"Oh," she said, as if being audited was a regular thing for her. "I'll let the doctor know you are here."

It was clear now what was happening. This clinic, which was about two blocks away from the pharmacy that processed all of the Dr. Bolo prescriptions, was being run (at least for the moment) by Maravilla. Maravilla was presenting himself as a full-fledged doctor. In fact, as a Physician's Assistant, Maravilla was legally authorized to write prescriptions under Dr. Bolo's supervision. But he was not free to take prescription pads, and start his own medical practice.

The minute Maravilla came out the door and saw me, he knew he was in trouble. But some people react to trouble differently than others. As a cop, I was used to physical danger: in the University, opponents usually take a more chicken-shit approach and try to ruin your career. At least when physical harm is the danger, you usually know where the punch is coming from. The career attack may be more acceptable in the university setting, but by no means is it any more civil.

With Maravilla, things were dicey. It could go either way. I expected more of a verbal assault, like I saw up at the Pediatrics clinic. Instead he came right at me, with a wide right hook. I remember thinking "Just what the hell does this guy think he's doing?" He was slow, and ill-prepared. His feet were too close together and so even with my bum knee I easily took a step to my right and gently pushed his body aside, taking advantage of his momentum. That momentum caused him to stumble head first into the door, and with a thunk he crumpled and went to the floor. I glanced over to the Rock, and she sat frozen, her mouth wide open.

I gave her a little shrug as if to say, "No, I don't understand this either - most of my audits aren't like this" and then turned my attention back to Maravilla. He was screaming at me in Spanish, hands holding his head. Blood was trickling down from a Z shaped wound on his forehead caused by the crash bar on the door. He looked like Harry Potter, only bloody stupid.

Contrary to what you've seen on TV, where heroes take blow after blow to the noggin and keep on fighting, most head injuries usually end the fight. Maravilla was clearly out of it. His yelling stopped and he was gritting his teeth in pain. His whole head was red with pain and rage, but mostly pain. I crouched over him to see where he had injured himself. Apparently he not only hit the door with his high forehead, he also scraped his face and arms as he hit the pavement. He was damn lucky the glass didn't break.

I turned again to the receptionist. "Call 911. He needs medical attention. Let's make sure we get a real doctor this time."

Chapter 28

The Vice Chancellor and I had a nice little chat. Basically, he reflected on my intelligence, I refrained from reflecting on his ancestry, and we got along swimmingly. He truly fits in with the environment, without the credentials. He has every trapping of a scholar, without actually being one. Tweed coat, patches on the elbows, red beard, and academic arrogance. All wrapped up in a self-important ball of crap that earns $136,000 of the taxpayers dollars, so he can spend weeks writing a single memo about a traffic light or some other half-assed bug up his butt.

"Just who the hell do you think you are, picking fights with our medical staff in public places!" VC Idiotface screamed.

Temper Dan. Temper.

"Look, I wasn't trying to fight anyone. He came at me. I was there finding out he was doing something wrong. Last time I checked my job description, that's what you hired me to do."

"Dan…" Marvin moaned from his rumpled seat in the corner.

I looked at him like he was being an idiot. He was. And he certainly was not defending me. On the force, the captain would go against the wall for you, no matter how stupid you had been. He would only humiliate you in private afterward. I was hoping for a little help.

"You can count on a lawsuit, and the Academic Senate wants your butt fired."

"That's bullshit." I said. "Those guys meet once a quarter. There hasn't been time for them to organize their feelings yet. You know what a touchy feely group they are." I was truly not helping my case.

"Gardner, I want this thimbleheaded auditor put on probation!"

Marvin just sighed heavily, and looked at me like I was a bad son.

"Marvin."

"Dan, go home."

When plan A doesn't work, most people go with plan B. Maravilla filed a complaint against me for assaulting him and harassing him outside of the workplace. For good measure, he also played the race card. Marvin was called to countless meetings with our Provost and the President of the University. Everyone was sure I needed extensive sensitivity training. I was pulled from the audit, and LaVonne had to complete the Pediatrics report by herself, and I was suspended for two weeks without pay. In other words, in order to punish me, they gave me a vacation. I helped LaVonne anyway, via email.

So I found myself by my pool a couple of days later with Shar, and I told her the whole story.

"LaVonne wound up writing the report with the finding that prescriptions were not adequately controlled, and Pediatrics was for a short time in danger of losing its HIPPA certification. Maravilla was arrested a couple days later and Scott Thomason wrote up an article about how the University "allowed" an illegal clinic to be run in Santa Ana run by one of our Physician's Assistants."

"Didn't they try to get any information from the University," Shar asked?

"Oh. Sure. Maxine Davis, legal counsel for the University, was quoted, in our defense, but her quote was buried in the second to the last paragraph. Most of the article concentrated on quotes by Maravilla, saying how he was forced to open a free-clinic because his community needed him. In his eyes, he was totally justified because his culture viewed him as a true physician."

"I don't know, but since he raised the cultural issue, I have to say I've seen that in my line of work as well." Shar hesitated. "Like it or not, different racial cultures think in different ways. I see a big difference between my clients, and there are some cultural patterns. By and large, our Latin men are usually very machisimo, and political correctness aside, sexist."

"What about older white guys like me?" I asked.

"Well, to be honest Dan, I don't get a lot of Boy Scouts," she countered with a sly grin. Damn. Once again I was a boy scout. "No, actually, guys like you are very paternal. Protective, like you tend to get with me."

"So you think Maravilla might really believe what he's saying?"

"It makes sense, if you think about it. Again, he's the authority figure. He sees it as his duty to take his medical training to his community." Then she hesitated. "But I must be wrong, because if that's so, wouldn't it come up more often? Maravilla isn't the world's first Latino physician's assistant."

"No, but whenever we talk about fraud in audit terms, we always say there are lots of factors needed for fraud to happen. One is opportunity. Maravilla had it. Another is motivation. That's Maravilla's internal need for people to respect him, in spite of his sour temper. He does it all the time. He gives out candy bars. He chats with patients. He wants respect, and when he doesn't think he's getting it, he tries to force it by yelling or punching. But what makes him different is that he just has an ethical standard that allows him to justify his actions for his cause. That's what makes him able to do what few others would try."

The last part of the article I could have written myself, because all OC Gazette articles about the University end with a paragraph summarizing a scandal we had five years ago, even though that story has nothing to do with the current situation reported. True to form, it read like this:

"The latest development is just one more incident the troubled University has experienced, starting with the donated organs scandal five years ago. Since that time, University management has struggled to regain control of the program where records were lost and employees were threatened with job loss for whistle blowing. Dr. Keith Balantine, a key figure of that scandal, has reestablished a practice in Buenos Aires, beyond the reach of local authorities."

"First of all," I said defensively, "we aren't a troubled environment, and we aren't struggling to regain control. The fact that the organ scandal came to light was because our internal control system was working. One Doctor ran a shoddy office, and when an employee raised the issue, he ignored it. She took the next step, and came to us in audit. We investigated. We took her report seriously. That's how it goes. It only became a scandal when someone, and I am not saying who, took the story to the Gazette, who loved the sensational side of donated organs being sold on the black market. There were lots of quotes from distraught relatives of organ donors; lots of drama and angst."

"But of course, that is awful, Dan. People need the assurance that when they make a living gift to the University for research, that the gift is used as it is intended."

"I agree wholeheartedly Shar, but when we learned of the one man's practice, we moved quickly to stop it. He was wrong, and used a loophole in our system for his own profit. But what people fail to realize is that to some degree, we have to trust our employees to do the right thing. It is impossible to control every situation from the front end. It isn't healthy to do that. It isn't economically feasible."

I reflected on what I just said. Running a University isn't all that unlike running any business. You have to control things as best you can to bring the amount of risk you face to point that you can live with. So, we trusted Dr. Balantine, just as we had trusted Maravilla, to do their jobs correctly and not engage in activities for their own profit. Unfortunately, here were two cases who betrayed that trust.

Shar summarized; "So Maravilla's personality, coupled with the opportunity provided to him by your trust, made it possible for him to run a clinic, providing a service. Manual Maravilla saw himself as a hero, and rallied support for his cause by whipping up outrageous claims in the media."

"Of course, bad journalists like Scott Thomason, are always glad to oblige, not realizing how they are really being used," I mused. "They don't have sufficient skills to be able to get the whole story straight before going to press. They write the emotional story, not the real one."

"But one thing troubles me," I continued. "Granted Maravilla was writing illegal prescriptions, and exposing Dr. Bolo, Pediatrics, the University and trusting patients to all kinds of risk. But with the exception of Corina Zavala, no one else was harmed. His prescriptions were all correct calls."

"Well, that one death is pretty significant, Dan."

"Yes, except for one thing. Corina didn't die from an allergic reaction to Zantac. It was a combination of Zantac and evidently some recreational drug, or other substance, which is way out of her personality."

"Such a combination could have happened to any physician."

"Right. So what, and who, really killed Corina?" Then I added, "and why?"

Chapter 29

LaVonne had called me and invited me to her house for dinner.

"I felt badly about how you got targeted to take the fall for this thing," she said. I was part of it too."

"No. You did normal audit functions. I'm the one who got it all muddied up by going to the drug store, and tailing Maravilla."

"Yes, but I'm the one who asked you to help the Zavalas."

"By George, you're right!" I said. "Seriously, no, I don't blame you at all. My actions are what got me in trouble. I'm lucky I still have a job."

"You have a job because you are a good auditor, and Marvin knows it."

"Hey, speaking of Marvin, do you have any idea what his wife's first name is? I've been racking my brain and I can't remember."

"Nope. We've never even talked about her. All I've ever heard is "the wife.""

"You too, eh?"

LaVonne fixed a great dinner, and we talked for a bit, about how the Zavala's found out how Corina was associated with the scandal when they heard about the neighborhood clinic. It was then that they discovered her prescription bottle, with Dr. Bolo's name, filled at the same pharmacy that was in the news report.

Surprisingly, there was a knock at the door. It was the Zavalas. I was surprised by their composure. They had every right to be bitter toward us, as University employees. But Adeline crossed the room and hugged me, and gave LaVonne a kiss on the cheek. Luis took my elbow in his left hand as we shook hands.

"We were driving by and we saw your car out front, Mr. Martyn," Said Luis. "I wanted to express my regret for what has happened to you. It seems to me you have been punished for trying to help us clear our daughter's reputation."

"No," I said. "I owe you an apology. Because of the way things came down, your daughter's name will forever be associated with this scandal."

"You misunderstand how we feel," said Luis. "We see no dishonor in Corina's association with that. She did nothing wrong. She was merely victimized by Maravilla. It is not a shameful association. If anything, it testifies to the extent that Corina trusted the people with whom she associated."

I was surprised to learn that the Zavalas had no intention to file a lawsuit.

"It is a question of honor, said Luis. "Turning Corina's death into a monetary value would dishonor the value of her life, and he said it would serve no positive purpose.

"And we so much appreciate how you tried to help us," added Adeline. "For you to be punished and for us to profit would be an insult to you."

"But I wouldn't..." I started to say.

"No," Luis said. "University representatives, you and LaVonne, were quick to help us, even before we knew you would be involved. In spite of what occurred, and the order of events, you acted in friendship and kindness, and at your own disadvantage. It would be wrong to profit off of your kindness."

I was amazed. In a strange way, the media had given the Zavala's what they wanted; a removal of any association of wrongdoing by Corina. Even though she was tied to the University scandal, Corina was no longer associated with her cocaine packaging boyfriend, and that was a positive turn of fate. The Zavala's said goodbye, and LaVonne chatted for a few more minutes before I left.

Chapter 30

I still felt unsettled. Even though the Zavala's had a sense of closure about Corina's death, I knew different. I had to know what killed her. I picked up my cell phone and called Steve Partaine.

"Hey Stretch. How you enjoying your vacation?"

"Not at all. I hate to call this late but I was wondering, did the Coroner ever come up with a definitive answer to what was in Corina Zavala's system?"

"Jeez, Stretch. Aren't you in enough trouble yet? Don't you think you'd be better off leaving well enough alone?"

"I'm a glutton for punishment, what can I say. What did you hear?'"

Nothin.' Zavala died of heart failure, because of a reaction to antihistamines. The Coroner didn't think it was sufficient to pursue further. You guys had a guy writing illegal prescriptions. What more do we need? Even if we could identify additional substances, Maravilla illegally wrote the antihistamine portion of the alleged combination. He's guilty as hell. We're nailing Maravilla's butt to the wall for running an illegal clinic and when we subpoenaed all the Drug-co records, we have proof he wrote Zavala's prescription. There is very good chance he'll get at least an Involuntary Manslaughter charge added as well tomorrow, if not Murder Two."

"OK, I'm happy as hell with that Steve, but I just have this need to know. So if you can't tell me, I'll just keep asking around. Where can I find Guttierez?"

"Oh cripes, Stretch..."

"C'mon. Besides. He should love to see me. I helped him get charged with a lesser crime that you guys blew anyway. So now we've gotta be pals."

"This kid hasn't got any pals, pal. And he never had any idea what role you played."

"An address, Steve."

"Listen citizen Martyn. I'm not giving you any address. I'm sworn to protect and serve. This isn't Rockford files. You can't call old police pals to get information so you can go over and incite a fight. Right about now, your standing in that community is somewhat sullied."

"Sullied? You actually use the word sullied?"

"Yeah, and I'm about to use a few more that you may be more familiar with. Do not seek out Guttierez. Do not endanger your job. Let us figure the whole thing out. We are actually pretty good at this stuff."

"So good you ignore half the case? If you ignore the combining ingredient to Corina's death, you may as well hand Maravilla's attorney the case, because he'll get his client off with the loophole. You and I both need to know. You for your case, me because I can't let it go."

"We're only going on the antihistamine. She had a reaction to Zantac. If you think the other stuff she ingested had anything to do with it, look into it. But we seriously doubt it. Your guy wrote one prescription too many. That's it. Goodbye Stretch."

Chapter 31

I drove to Iglesia de Dios. It was locked, of course. It was a late summer evening. But there was a sign on the door, and the sign said that in the event of an alarm, call (714) 555-2143. I took a chance and it paid off. The voiced that answered was familiar.

"Is this Pastor Ricardo Cruz?" I asked.

"Yes. How may I help you?" came his rich baritone voice.

I made my request, and he said he'd do what he could do. About fifteen minutes later, a well lit Chevy truck with dark windows pulled up. Behind that, a nondescript white sedan parked and Pastor Ric Cruz jumped out. As he greeted me, the driver of the first vehicle got out, and joined us. I thanked Pastor Cruz for getting in contact with him. It was Ramon Guttierez.

"Let us go inside." Said Cruz, and he unlocked the door to the church. And then Cruz went to the side door.

He unlocked it, and in marched about 15 more gang members. Clearly, Ramon wanted support.

I was struck by the fact that they were all various ages. Some as young as Ramon, but a couple others looked at least over 40. Each of them sported their tattooed initials somewhere visibly, the letters depicted in bones. Lots of other graphic images were tattooed as well.

They filed in, and Cruz invited me to sit. I sat in a pew, Ramon sat next to me, and the rest of the Bones gang sat all around us. Cruz stood in front, and leaned against the rail.

Intimidated? Me? Currently beloved by the Hispanic community? You betcha.

"Corina Zavala's death affected us all," Cruz began to explain to me. "To understand the inner workings of the world from our viewpoint, you have to understand that Southern California has been a volatile place for our people from the very beginning. We are talking centuries of struggle."

I nodded in understanding. The indigenous people of the area were originally the Gabriolino tribes. Western Europe found great value in establishing footholds in the western most part of the continent. The value of establishing trade routes in a land where the native people were primarily agricultural was a whole new way of thinking about the west. The Spanish came. The English came. They brought their religion, and mixed their DNA into the local population. They built cities and fought over land, water and who would govern. The fights were both fair and unfair glorious and evil. In the end, the identity of the people who lived here became mixed and unclear. Consequently, trying to establish an identity to hold, the new Mexican Americans struggled and fought corrupt leaders and landowners, the holders of land grants, ill advised regarding the future of the land. Through it all, the workers remained in agriculture, especially in the rich farmlands of Orange County.

Slowly, and continuing to this day, the interests in the west found other financial benefits. The Pacific Rim beckoned, and industries flocked to an area where the sun always shone and snow seldom stopped business. It wasn't necessary to train the locals; they had their culture, and work in the fields. Surely there was plenty of room for all.

But the land is finite, and in an amazingly short amount of time, those who lacked the language and culture of the east coast were marginalized. Cities plowed the fields, and the grids of streets followed the old wind breaking rows of eucalyptus. The farms disappeared, and with it, the Mexican American's means for financial support. Too late, the need for education was recognized, leaving behind a wide sector of the population with nowhere to go, and little promise for the future. These were the people that got caught in the web of the lacework; the grids that made up Southern California.

"Ramon has had a great struggle, as you well know, Mr. Martyn. He has made mistakes. And his life was dangerously close to destruction."

"But I had Corina," said Ramon.

The gang stirred. One of them touched Ramon's shoulder.

Cruz continued.

"Corina was like that. She was always aiming for excellence, hoping for the best, and believing that anyone in her life could live a wonderful life. She helped them see beyond their problems. She helped friends with their grades. She helped them find jobs. If they had any deficit, Corina worked to be the element to cancel their flaw. She truly believed that with the right attitude, any obstacle could be overcome."

And then for the first time, I realized that none of these guys surrounding me were here about me. They were here for Ramon.

"Corina was so... incredible," said Ramon. She believed in me, and believed I could be better than where I was going. She got me to thinking, and so I thought if I could just score one good thing, just once, I could start turning my life around."

It was then that I became aware of one particular member of the Bones, the one who had patted Ramon on the shoulder. He was one of the older members, and wore a leather vest that left his arms exposed. On his left arm sported his Bones I.D, his initials, Z.A. made from bone images. A knife was depicted separating the two letters.

"Corina was far more than anyone has said in the news," Z.A. said. She has known most of us a long time. We work hard to make people fear us, but Corina never did. She was always fearless. Even as."

"Even as we all tried to be feared" interrupted another. He exchanged glances with Z.A.

"Ramon, what happened the night she died?" I asked.

"I swear to you, I have no idea. She had been so busy preparing for graduation. She was wearing herself out. The day she died, she was in high gear, in spite of her allergies. I know she was taking something for them. I just figured she was tired from the side effects."

"And you don't know of anything else she ingested?" I asked.

Ramon looked at Cruz, as if to say "He doesn't believe me." Then he looked at me with piercing, convincing eyes.

"I told you before; I know of no other thing Corina ingested. I gave her nothing. She hadn't even eaten at the party."

The kid's eyes filled with tears. Z.A. looked down.

"Corina just... died."

"OK," I said. "I get it. In fact, you may find this hard to believe, and think I am just saying this because you have me outnumbered here 16 to one, but I believed you at OCLU."

Ramon was taken aback.

"In fact, I think I just about have this whole thing figured out. I just need to check one more thing."

There was again, a stir among the Bones, and while I was fairly certain that Cruz wasn't going to allow them to cut me up into pieces there in the sanctuary, I now also believed I might even make it back to my car.

Now, I just had to prove one more thing.

Chapter 32

I was at the end. I had followed every lead I knew.

It was ten o'clock, but I needed a favor. I called LaVonne. She was still up. I asked if I could come back for a bit. She said yes, it was fine. She had been watching television.

I drove down 17th one more time. Sure enough, the guy with the signs was still in front of Santa Ana College. Even at 10:00, there he was; red faced and smiling under a straw hat. It was probably almost time to go, but he was there, waiting astride his bicycle. Waiting for one last message for me?

"What your friends don't know
Might kill you.
Goodbye"

"Man, isn't that the truth," I said, as I turned the corner.

Well, close to the truth. I honked my horn, and gave him a thumbs-up sign.

When I knocked on her door, LaVonne answered immediately.

"Got a computer with internet access?" I asked.

"Good to see you again too," she responded. She took me to the den and in a few minutes, I was beyond reasonably assured that my theory might be correct.

"I think I know what, and who, killed Corina Zavala." I announced.

LaVonne was stunned.

"You mean, it wasn't Maravilla?"

"Well, yes, kind of. But he wasn't alone. I need your help to prove it."

I made a call to Partaine, and he told me he would get right on my suggestion. I also told Lavonne what I wanted her to do.

Chapter 33

I sat outside the Drug-co in my car. After a few minutes, LaVonne came out, and got in the car.

"Got it," she announced.

Perfect. One more stop.

We went to the Main Place mall, and once again, LaVonne went inside, again returning with a package. "All done" she said, and I gave her a sideways glance to confirm our now shared knowledge. She giggled. "I never knew undercover work could be such a rush," she said.

The next morning, I awaited a call back from Partaine. "You were right Stretch," said Partaine. "The coroner verified it this morning."

I made some other calls, and LaVonne and I drove to the Zavalas.

Partaine's unmarked car was sitting in their driveway. He was standing on the porch, just as the Zavalas were opening the door. They welcomed all of us, and we all went into the living room where Theresa was already seated.

There was a knock at the back door, and in walked Pastor Ricardo Cruz with Ramon Guttierez and Z.A. To say Adeline and Luis were surprised would be an understatement. Their emotions exploded.

"What are you doing here!" Luis demanded.

But he was addressing the older gang member.

"I invited him," I said. "because I believe he needs to hear this. After all, Corina was his daughter too."

If Partaine and LaVonne could have been knocked over with a feather, this was the moment. Adeline and Luis stood together, separated from the rest of the room. Cruz positioned himself in between them and Ramon, and Corina's birth-father, Zacarias Armindarez.

"OK, I think this might be easier if we all sit down," I said.

"Where to begin," I started. "We all know that Corina was a very unusual woman. She was always able to see the best in everyone, sometimes surprising the people who knew her best."

"And she was an achiever. Corina faced many an obstacle, and met it head on. Fearless. Corina was always certain not only would she come out fine, but so would those she loved. Her academic achievements matched her curiosity, and she applied an unfaltering faith to everything she dreamed."

"So it should come as no surprise to anyone that she would apply her curiosity to find her birth father, which, I assume Zacarias, she did at a very early age."

"That's right, but how did you figure me.?"

"The other night, at Iglesia de Dios, you started to talk, and I thought it was unusual that the eldest member of the gang would inject himself into Corina's world so personally. You started to tell me how fearless she was, and were about to say ever since she was a child, until the other guy interrupted you. before you gave away your secret. But the damage was already done. Your tattoo initials, "Z.A." told me who you were. Zacarias isn't the most common name out there."

"Corina sought me out when she was twelve," he said, and an audible gasp came out of Adeline. "She had found a picture of me in her mother's bedroom, and started showing it around. It wasn't too long before someone recognized me, and sent her my way."

"You abandoned her!" said Adeline.

"True, but I could see my life was heading where I didn't want her to be. Ten years later, when she sought me out, I couldn't turn away again. She got to know me, and my friends, and grew up with many of them as the second wave of Bones came from her classmates. She had no fear of us, because I was her father. But I also made it very clear to her: keep a straight life. Don't follow my example. Make your mother proud of you. And she loved you very much. And you too, Luis. You raised her well."

"So," I continued, "Corina continued on, loving, and hoping, and dreaming that anything was possible. She studied, graduated with honors, and won a scholarship."

"But it doesn't all happen as a picture book. You can't control everyone she meets, as you are now fully aware. Along the line, she began to search for ways to cope with some of her everyday stresses. At this point, knowing the people Corina knew, it is amazing she didn't turn to drugs.

"I never would have allowed it." Armindariz spat out.

"Sounds noble, but I wonder how many other kids you DID allow it to happen to," snapped Adeline.

I held up my hand.

"Folks, please. We're not here about that," I said, though if you missed the tension between Armindariz and Partaine in the room, you would have to be brain dead. Corina wasn't any different that almost anyone else I've meet in Auditing. Lots of people have motive, and opportunity to do the wrong thing, but they just don't cross the line. Corina just wasn't going to do it, and not wanting to go the drug route, looked for more acceptable supplements to help her out."

All eyes turned to Theresa, who worked in the health food store.

Chapter 34

Theresa was shocked.

"You mean, I gave her something that killed her?"

"Did you give her anything?!" Luis demanded.

"Well, um." Theresa began to cry. "Yes. But it was all over-the-counter herbs and stuff. Nothing that would kill her. Did I?"

"No, Theresa," I said. "You didn't give her anything that killed her. Though sad to say, it could have. She may have first come to you for certain things she heard advertised on the radio." and with that, I took the bag from LaVonne, and pulled out a bottle of "Focus-Smart."

"Remember when LaVonne came in yesterday? I asked her to go in and buy this from you. It is just one of several supplemental products available marketed to people who want to increase their ability to concentrate. You ever sell anything like this to Corina?"

"That's exactly the stuff," Theresa replied.

I went on. "To Corina, it was no different than drinking an energy drink, or a vitamin supplement. Its actual value is debatable, but that's how this stuff gets marketed."

"Which brings us to the final piece of the puzzle; LaVonne made one other purchase yesterday." I took the other bag from her, and pulled out a bottle with Chinese lettering on it.

"Ever see this stuff before? A few years ago, you could buy it in the store where you worked, Theresa. It's an herbal supplement, called "Ma Huang," in Southeast Asia. You might have heard of it as Ephedra.

Ephedra is another supplement that lots of health stores used to sell as an energy booster, allergy relief and diet enhancer. But as it turns out, Ephedra is now prohibited for sale. Proponents of it say it's safe, but research has linked it to at least 50 deaths. It was outlawed in the 1990's. Remember the diet supplement called Fen-Phen? A form of Ephedra was part of the mix. And Ephedra turns especially toxic when mixed. with allergy medications."

Everyone in the room was stunned. Partaine's phone rang, and he took it into the kitchen.

"Thinking back on the night of Corina's death, all the elements were there. Corina's allergies were acting up. She had been stressed with finals, and plans for graduation. She had been running errands, including picking up her Zantac prescription that Maravilla wrote for her at Drug-co. She probably struck up a conversation with the nice, trustworthy pharmacist behind the counter, a sweet old woman of Asian descent. Theresa told her about her allergies, her stress, and needed just one more energy boost to get her through the party."

Partaine entered the room. "Right again, Stretch. DEA just found a nice stash of Ephedra behind the counter at Drug-co, along some other pretty interesting treats. I guess the old lady was passing out her old remedies on the side."

Turns out the pharmacist had been a doctor in Vietnam, and came over after the fall, with hundreds of others. Unlicensed in the USA, she opted instead to become a pharmacist, which takes just a little less study as becoming a physician. Santa Ana has lots of Vietnamese residents from that era, and she had been supplying them with some of their old-world solutions.

I looked across the room. Adeline was crying in Luis' arms, as LaVonne stood nearby. TA just sat in silence, looking at the floor. Theresa and Ramon went outside. Partaine made more phone calls.

I wanted a sense of satisfaction. But the room was too full of broken hearts.

Chapter 35

Maravilla had a lousy attorney and never grasped the impact of the Ephedra element. Maravilla was convicted of Involuntary Manslaughter. He continued to get paid though, right up to the day of his conviction.

Universities are often scared to stop paying people.

About a year later, and in direct relation to our scandal, the State of California changed its law regarding Physician's Assistants writing prescriptions. Both names, the PA and the Doctor, have to appear on the form, and are printed on the bottle. It definitely cut down on liability claims against specific doctors, but there is still no control on pharmacies filling prescriptions, insofar as verifying the prescription is genuinely prescribed. Some voluntarily double-check with the issuing physician. Others, usually the smaller, non-chain ones, don't bother. Given the right circumstances, people could make up their own prescription pads on the computer, have it filled by a less reputable pharmacy, and voila. Prozac for everyone.

Scott Thomason turned his original article into an expose series of University wrongdoing, beginning two days later in the Gazette, though arrests had already been made, and everything was sewn up. Of course, the community was shocked. The Gazette planned to follow up with anyone who contacted them, that might have also had a prescription filled at Drug-co by Maravilla as Bolo. They milked it for months. He must have relished adding my name to the list of people involved. He won a best journalism award from some newspaper group for uncovering the mess. The guy is a genius. Once again, we looked stupid. Lawsuits ensued. Pediatrics managed to keep its teaching certification, but lost a good Pediatric surgeon. Bolo decided to get out of Orange County and relocate to a university in Massachusetts.

The University was embarrassed and just hoping the whole thing would blow over. LaVonne never got into any trouble, and amazingly, Marv went to bat for me, and saved my job. "Dan Martyn was doing everything he could to ensure proper ethical procedures and internal controls for our academic and research interests." I love it when he gets all Audit-sounding.

I was put back into service, though they never actually stopped paying me while I was "off the payroll." We've been all through that. I had to attend sensitivity classes, though it could be argued that I am the most sensitive guy that ever graced their halls. Even so, Marv gave me what he considered only the safest assignments. I was bored for months, until. well, that's another story for another time.

At least I managed to salvage something from the event. Karen Taylor called me one afternoon to talk about it, and we meet for dinner. She was gracious, and terrific. And I was a boy scout. Honest.

Epilogue

The forty days were over.

"My work here is done.

Time to move on. Tomorrow will be the new day. Think I'll move west. This is a big web. I have new insights. New plans. I have new signs to make.

The message... that's what's important. Teach the people. Make them think. Stir them to life. That's the important thing. I'll be here.

Summer is better. More people. No more rain. When it rains, they stay inside. Not me. It doesn't really matter to me. I'll be here."

The duffle bag over his back, he balanced himself with his sign and headed back east on 17th toward home. Traffic was light late at night. Getting home is easier.

As he started to take off, a driver passing by honked the horn and gave the "thumbs-up" sign.

He nodded his head, without smiling.

"Good. Someone understood."

**Read on for a preview of the next Dan Martyn
Audit mystery novel by Robert A. Clemmons**

Audits are Terrifying

Mike O'Hagen was thinking once again of his Navy days. Thirty years ago, he served his country in the U.S. Navy, proudly aboard the USS Kittyhawk, the proudest super carrier in the fleet. Newer ships have come, and the Kittyhawk was now gone, but not a day went by that O'Hagan didn't remember with fondness the daily mix of ocean brine and machine oil in the air.

This afternoon air was fresh as he arrived to begin shift at the university's pumping station. He considered himself lucky to have scored this lucrative gig working for the State of California, in the heart of Orange County. He liked most of his coworkers, loved the eucalyptus trees surrounding his workplace, and though the pay wasn't the highest he could earn in the county, Mike knew the security and job benefits couldn't be beaten.

O'Hagen worked the first night shift, beginning at 6:00 P.M., just as most of the campus activity was coming to a close. Most of the campus office buildings were closed for business at 5:00 P.M., and only the night classes and special events brought visitors to the campus.

From a mechanical aspect, few campuses in America, or even the world, were built like this one. The entire campus was build around a central park; a wide open area of grass, hills, rolling lawns, and pathways. Around the entire park was a wide walkway, and coming out from the center of the circle radiated the spokes of educational divisions; Humanities, Social Sciences, Engineering, Chemistry, Medicine.

But only a few knew, or paid much attention to what lay beneath that walkway. It was what kept O'Hagen working for the Governor. Beneath the greenery was a tunnel, containing miles and miles of pipes. High temperature water pipes, chilled water pipes, compressed air pipes, waste water pipes, utility pipes. All of the pipes circled the campus, carrying their contents to each of the educational and administrative buildings surrounding the ring.

The chilled water provided cooling to buildings. The high temperature water lines provided heat. Waste lines serviced the rest rooms and other campus waste. The entire network of pipes formed a spider-like maze in ever-growing complexity in the tunnels beneath the walkway. With every study discipline group of buildings, a spoke tunnel would branch off the main tunnel. It was a labyrinth of ugliness beneath the beauty above.

Mike O'Hagen arrived just as some of the equipment functions began to change. It was fall, and the heat of the day was beginning to bow to the cool ocean breezes that came up from Newport Beach. Buildings required less cooling, and it was time to begin drawing some of the system water that cooled the campus back into the enormous Thermal Energy Storage Tank (TEST).

"Mike. Are we glad to see you. We've got a problem," said Pete Walker, manager of the pumping station.

"What's up?"

"We think there is a problem with the TEST," said Walker. "The discharge pressure has been low all day. We just couldn't get the volume we needed."

Mike wasn't happy. What that meant was that something was blocking the discharge valve, and that had to mean that something inside the tank, probably scale build up, broke loose, fell to the bottom, and plugged the hole.

But the TEST should have been scale-free.

The TEST was O'Hagan's baby. When the campus was searching for ways to reduce the cost of energy, it was O'Hagan that suggested building the enormous tank. At first, it met with objections, because, well, it wasn't very pretty. But when O'Hagan showed them how much money they could save by tanking the water that had been warmed during the day, and cooling it during the night when energy rates were a fraction of the daytime rates, O'Hagan became a hero.

So the six story tank found a home, nestled among the eucalyptus trees, against a hillside on campus. A large armadillo graced the side in a display of campus spirit: the lowly armadillo was the campus mascot. During the night, the water was quickly and cheaply chilled, and the next day, as buildings began to heat up, water was drawn from the tank through the miles of pipes to the air conditioning systems for each of the campus study building groups.

"Shi... I can't believe it," said O'Hagen. "What the hell are we paying the water quality people for, if they can't keep the system scale free? Have you begun refilling it?"

"No," replied Walker. "We're just pushing the water through the cooling towers for now, like we used to before the TEST." We thought you'd like to check it out."

Before the TEST was built, the cooling water in the system just stayed in the pipe loops, pumping in a circle around the ring, passing through the cooling towers on each pass by the pumping plant. It was an open-air system, and the water fell in a series of tiny waterfalls from the top to bottom. By the time it got to the bottom of the cooling towers, the temperature drop was significant. But not nearly enough to supply the demand considering the current size of the campus.

"Yeah, I guess I better head up the ladder."

So O'Hagan began the long arduous climb. On the back side of the tank was a six-story ladder broken down in two-story series. It was surrounded by a safety cage, to provide the climber some sense of safety as he made his way to the top of the TEST. It was, however, just an illusion. Any slip, and the climber would certainly fall straight down, not out, and possibly break his leg in the rungs.

It took O'Hagen twenty minutes to negotiate the ladder. Back in his Kittyhawk days, he could have done it faster... he probably would have had to make it faster. But it had been a long time, and his tool belt made him feel like Mother Earth had her hands around him, pulling him ground ward. The last few steps were killer.

At the top, he rested a bit on the platform, and then made his way over to the hatch.

"See anything?" Walker's voice crackled through the radio on his tool belt.

"Just a sec," said O'Hagen, "I haven't opened the hatch yet."

He fumbled through his keys, and found the right one for the lock. "That's odd," he thought, noticing that the lock was missing. Gripping the wheel, he slowly turned it hand over hand, and lifted the heavy hatch door to the left.

There was no pressure in the tank. He didn't expect any rush of air. And it was dark. The dusk was beginning to settle on the campus, and the tank was empty, pitch dark.

The pumps were off, and the water was dark and still. He took a mag light from his tool belt, and peered through the water.

What he saw, made his stomach lurch.

"OH GOD. Oh god oh god oh god!"

Walker could hear him below without the radio.

"What? WHAT?" Pete yelled into the radio.

But Mike wasn't listening. He was dizzy. Disoriented. Already out of breath from the climb, he stumbled on the platform, nearly falling down the ladder casement.

He fell to his knees, and looked again into the TEST.

The body was female, naked, black hair, and obviously very, very cold. Blue in color. She was severely misshapen and broken, her torso bending in ways unimaginable.

O'Hagen looked closer; Bloated and ugly from the water exposure, she had obviously been in the tank when the pumps came on, and had been sucked down to the bottom, blocking the discharge line. Her fingers were bloody; some missing. She must have been there all day, as the water rushed over her. At first, she must have struggled frantically, trying to push away from the grate.

"OH God."

"Mike, what the hell is wrong? I'm coming up."

By the time he had climbed to the top, Pete found his sobbing engineer kneeling at the hatchway hedge, motionless. He looked down and saw the body.

Taking the radio from his side, he signaled the plant office.

"Plant Office, this is Plant One."

"Go ahead" said the voice over the radio.

"Plant Office, call campus police over to the TEST. We have a situation."